THE ITALIAN'S
RUTHLESS
MARRIAGE
COMMAND

THE ITALIAN'S RUTHLESS MARRIAGE COMMAND

BY

HELEN BIANCHIN

™MILLS & BOON®

First published in Great Britain 2009
Large Print edition 2009
Harlequin Mills & Boon Limited,
Eton House, 18-24 Paradise Road,
Richmond, Surrey TW9 1SR

© Helen Bianchin 2009

ISBN: 978 0 263 20611 1

Set in Times Roman 16½ on 18½ pt.
16-0809-45607

Harlequin Mills & Boon policy is to use papers that are
natural, renewable and recyclable products and made
from wood grown in sustainable forests. The logging and
manufacturing process conform to the legal environmental
regulations of the country of origin.

Printed and bound in Great Britain
by CPI Antony Rowe, Chippenham, Wiltshire

CHAPTER ONE

'Do I *have* to go to kindergarten today?'

Taylor drew the dark-haired little boy close in a loving hug, felt his small arms curve round her neck in a gesture that tugged at her heart…and fiercely vowed to protect him at any cost.

Just three and a half years old, he'd had his world recently shattered beyond belief with the loss of both his parents in a car crash.

Ben d'Alessandri had become part of her life from the moment her sister, Casey, had announced her pregnancy.

Together, they'd shared setting up a nursery, choosing motifs, soft toys and baby clothes…indulgently sanctioned by Casey's husband, Leon.

It had been Taylor who'd gowned up and added her encouragement to that of Leon as they supported Casey during the birthing process…and afterwards, witnessing Casey and Leon's shared joy in the miracle of their baby son.

Two sisters, tragically orphaned in their teens, they'd shared a close bond, championing each other in their chosen pursuits…and celebrating the other's successes. Casey had graduated in law and Taylor, a talented writer, had had her first book accepted for publication a year before Ben's birth.

'Why can't I come with you and see Zio Dante?'

The mere mention of Leon's brother's name caused Taylor's stomach to do a slow backward flip before settling into a state of unease.

'You'll see your uncle soon,' she said gently, meeting his solemn gaze.

'Promise?'

'Yes.' It was a given.

'Today?'

'I think so,' she allowed cautiously. 'Except we must remember he's had a long flight from Italy, and he's going straight to a business meeting.'

Ben nodded his head. 'With you.'

'Uh-huh.'

'About me.'

Oh, Lord, honesty to his level of understanding seemed the best way to go.

'Of course,' she teased. 'Aren't you just the most important person in the universe? A boy for whom your devoted aunt will slay dragons?'

'And lions.'

Taylor placed her lips into the curve of his neck and blew a soft raspberry kiss, heard him giggle and brushed her lips to his cheek, loving the clean smell of soap, shampoo and freshly laundered clothes.

'The entire animal kingdom if I had to,' she assured solemnly and joined in his delighted laughter.

'Zio Dante, too?'

It was all too easy to picture Dante in *hero* mode. His tall, broad-shouldered frame exuded male perfection, but it was his strong-boned facial features which drew attention.

Eyes dark as sin and just as dangerous, they alternately promised or threatened much.

The first time she'd met him had been the night of Casey and Leon's engagement party when he had flown in from New York for the celebration.

All it had taken was a look, and the blood had fizzed in her veins, causing her emotions to go every which way as she fought against the instant electric attraction. Something which stole the breath from her throat and any coherent words from her mind.

He was a man who made her think of the forbidden. And how he could easily circumvent a woman's objection…especially hers.

Except she'd consciously guarded herself against him, sensing that he *knew* she did so, for she'd been sure the teasing touch of his mouth to her own had been deliberate at the evening's end.

The light sweep of his tongue along her lower lip, the faint nibble at its sensitive centre…and how the action caused her body to suffuse with languorous warmth.

'Taylor?'

Oh, heavens, *get a grip*.

She made a dashing slash with one hand and summoned a fierce expression as she assured, 'Zio Dante will slay them all with his mighty sword.'

Ben's eyes grew round. 'Does he have a *real* sword?'

'No, just a pretend one.'

Taylor rose to her feet with Ben in her arms. 'Now, young man. It's kindergarten and lots of fun with the other kids. OK?'

'I guess.'

She collected her bag, keys, locked the small two-bedroom apartment and together they took the lift down to the underground car park, where her Lexus sedan stood in its parking bay.

It wasn't difficult to engage Ben's attention during the short drive and, although he appeared pensive as she checked him in with one of the carers, he brightened almost immediately as two of his friends raced over to greet him.

His smile and wave as she left tugged at her heartstrings, and she hated leaving him. Except it was imperative he maintain a routine after the tragic loss of his parents.

Poor little fellow. She'd guided him through the grief of losing his mummy and daddy, and made him feel as secure as humanly possible in the ensuing weeks as they had both attempted to come to terms with the tragedy.

His tears had flowed freely as she comforted

him…while her own were shed in the dark of night without comfort or solace of any kind.

Part of it was concern, Taylor admitted as she eased the Lexus into the flow of traffic heading into the city. When Casey and Leon had requested Taylor and Dante be Ben's legal guardians, should the worst ever happen, no one had ever thought that this time would come. Now Taylor wondered as to precisely how custody of Ben could be shared by two people who resided at opposite ends of the world.

She'd considered every scenario, agonised and lost sleep over each of them…*knowing* there was a need for mutual agreement, yet unable to countenance the success of any *one* solution.

There was the sinking, sickening feeling that Dante would exert unfair pressure, given Ben was a d'Alessandri heir.

A fierce protectiveness strengthened her resolve. If Dante attempted to remove Ben from her care, he'd have to do so over her dead body!

Dante d'Alessandri stepped down onto the tarmac from his Gulfstream jet, thanked the flight attendant, cleared Customs, then exited the terminal and crossed to the black Mercedes parked a few metres away. He acknowledged the chauffeur and slid into the rear seat, resting his head on the soft, buttery leather.

Within minutes the Mercedes eased towards the exit leading from Sydney's major air terminal.

Gusty showers dashed rain against the windscreen as the vehicle traversed the main arterial road leading into the city.

Fitting, perhaps, given events of the past few weeks wherein he'd dealt with his brother and sister-in-law's accidental death, accompanied his widowed mother from Florence to Sydney for the funeral, then had personally ensured her safe return to Italy.

Two brothers, Dante reflected, a few years apart in age, close during their formative years, through university, adhering to their father's dictate they each take a lowly position in the d'Alessandri corporation and work their way up. Something at which they'd both succeeded. It was Dante who had been selected to remain at the Italian head office while Leon was dispatched to the Australian corporate branch in Sydney.

Opposite sides of the world had lessened individual contact, but they'd kept in frequent touch via phone and email.

Now Dante was back in Sydney to settle Leon's affairs and deal with the legalities involved in sharing custody of his brother's son, who thankfully had been safely ensconced in kindergarten on the day his parents had been killed.

A child he'd promised to care for…and would, given he was legally bound to do so by the terms of Leon and Casey's wills.

Five years ago he'd stood as best man at the wedding of his younger brother to Casey Adamson, and upon Ben's birth a little over a year later he'd agreed to be named together with Casey's sister, Taylor, as Ben's legal guardian and godparent.

A protective measure, and one it had been hoped would never need to be put into effect, Dante ruminated with a pensive expression.

His eyes narrowed slightly as he recalled Taylor's image. Tall, slender, dark blonde hair.

A young woman he'd met at Leon's engagement, partnered at Leon's wedding, again at Ben's christening, and shared mutual support with at Leon and Casey's funeral.

He recalled the unshed tears glistening in her eyes during the service...the moment she faltered, then regained control during the reading of the eulogy. And afterwards as the family stood at the grave site, the cool autumn day and the wind whipping at her hair.

It had been Taylor, immediately following the fateful accident, who'd taken Ben into her care and shielded the child during the difficult weeks that followed.

Something for which he was immensely grateful, given his need to support his mother, tie up urgent business matters and delegate in order to facilitate his return to Sydney.

Dante checked his watch as the chauffeur drew the Mercedes to a halt at the kerb adjacent a tall city building.

It took only minutes to gain access to Leon's legal firm on a high floor, give his name and have the lawyer's PA lead him into a large executive office where Leon's legal representative welcomed him with a customary greeting before indicating the young woman who'd risen from her chair.

'Taylor,' Dante acknowledged as he closed the space between them, took her offered hand, then leant in and brushed his lips to her cheek, sensed the faint hitch in her breath...and wondered at it.

Her height was accentuated by stiletto-heeled boots, black fitted trousers and a mid-thigh-length knitted woollen jacket in air-force blue, hitched low over her hips by a wide leather belt.

His brief return to Florence had wrought a regular email exchange regarding their nephew and confirmation of today's legal consultation.

As sisters, he reflected, Taylor and Casey had shared an affectionate bond, but different personalities.

Casey, so bright and bubbly, with laughing eyes and a wicked sense of humour. Her personal world had been filled with her husband and son. Whereas Taylor adopted a reserved, almost wary mask he found intriguing.

Yet he'd seen it slip for a brief moment when

Casey had said her vows to Leon during their wedding ceremony. Later at Ben's christening, when Taylor had pledged to care for her nephew as his godmother...and recently at Casey and Leon's funeral service.

It was a vulnerability she'd endeavoured to hide...one which fascinated him on a fundamental level.

A woman it would give a man pleasure to tame...if only to peel back the various layers of her reserve and discover what lay in her heart. Possibly her soul.

A challenge, but not one he'd been inclined to pursue during his infrequent stopovers.

'Dante.'

Her voice held polite warmth, and he had the uncanny feeling she'd read his mind...something he seriously doubted.

As CEO and president of the d'Alessandri corporation, he'd gained a serious reputation for cool-headed, cut-throat negotiation...an essential requisite for wheeling and dealing in multinational commercial real estate on an annual multi-billion-dollar scale, with a personal fortune placing him among Europe's wealthy echelon.

Such a level of success hadn't been achieved without an ability to guard whatever strategy he chose to employ.

The lawyer indicated one of three comfortable chairs as he resumed his position behind the large desk. 'Please take a seat.' He pulled a file forward and opened it. 'The custody issue regarding Leon and Casey's son needs to be addressed. I assume you've each given it some thought?'

'Ben is comfortable living with me,' Taylor offered quietly. 'I work from home, so there are no issues with child care. I know Casey would have been happy for me to take primary responsibility.'

'I propose Ben should make his home with me in Italy—' Dante paused fractionally and offered Taylor a considering look '—where he can be educated and groomed to eventually take his place in the corporation my late father founded. Ben is a d'Alessandri heir, the first in his generation. I have no doubt Leon would want his son to follow in his family's footsteps.'

Taylor's stomach plummeted at the unvoiced

implication, and her eyes darkened with dismay. 'That can't be considered an option.'

Was that her voice? It sounded slightly strangled, even to her own ears. 'Ben is still struggling to comprehend the loss of his parents. He needs familiar surroundings and a regular routine. Not,' she added with increasing concern, 'be faced with adjusting to a strange country, people he doesn't know and a language he doesn't understand. It was never Casey's intention Ben live anywhere other than Sydney.'

'Nor, I imagine,' Dante drawled, 'was it Leon and Casey's desire to leave this earth at such a young age.' His eyes speared her own. 'But fate has chosen otherwise.'

She subjected him to an encompassing appraisal, noting his broad-boned facial features, startling dark eyes, the generous mouth...the wide shoulders beneath superb tailoring, his tall, lithe frame whose height surpassed her own by several inches.

He looked precisely the man he'd become... powerful, ruthless. Lethal. Not someone with whom to tangle.

Yet she'd seen him in a lighter mood, caught his smile, witnessed his warmth with Casey…the affectionate camaraderie he'd shared with Leon. His gentleness with Ben.

There had been a time when she'd felt at ease in his company and wondered if something more might develop between them, had it not been for an assault by an intruder a year after Ben's birth that had left her both physically and emotionally scarred…something which resulted in her avoiding a relationship with any man, especially a man as vital as Dante.

'You travel extensively,' Taylor pursued. 'How can you tuck him into bed each night and read him a bedtime story,' she protested, 'or be there to listen to his dreams and fears, hug him when he's sad and share his laughter?' She was on a roll, passionate in her concern and despairing of finding a solution to the adequate care of her dearly loved nephew.

'An alternative is for Ben to reside several months with you,' Dante offered, 'followed by equal time with me.'

The green flecks in her hazel eyes became more evident, and reminded Dante of the lush green foliage protecting the succulent grapes ripening in his Tuscan vineyard.

'How will uprooting him every few months provide him with any stability?' Taylor queried with agonised disbelief. 'He's just a little boy.'

'Who will receive the devoted adoration of his grandmother, and the care of a highly qualified nanny,' Dante informed with calm patience, and saw the pulse at the base of her throat quicken in agitation. 'I'm prepared to offer you open visitation rights, together with an all-expenses-paid trip to Florence,' he continued, 'including accommodation while Ben is in my care, to ensure your satisfaction he is happily ensconced in his new environment.'

Dante's voice held a subtle silkiness which she appeared to ignore, and he wondered if she knew the full extent of his power.

He regarded her carefully. 'Consideration for Ben's education must be addressed.' He paused fractionally, then offered, 'There is the option of a reputable boarding school.'

'No,' Taylor refuted swiftly.

There was a tense silence, one the lawyer attempted to breach with a placating spread of his hands, which Dante chose to ignore as Taylor fixed him with an appealing look.

'Is it of no consequence that I've had constant contact with Ben since he was born, and love him as much as if he were my own?'

Dante leant back in his chair and steepled his fingers. 'If this is so, I take it you're prepared to do anything to ensure his comfort, his happiness?'

He reminded her of a jungle cat, all lithe power and the ever-present threat of the moment he would strike.

'Yes,' she said without hesitation.

Dante subjected her to an unwavering scrutiny. 'Given neither of us will agree to sole custody with open visitation rights, do you have a sensible suggestion to offer?'

Hadn't she worried herself sick trying to come up with *sensible*…and failed miserably?

'Whatever decision we make *has* to benefit Ben.'

'On that we agree,' Dante revealed quietly as he shifted his attention to the lawyer. 'The wills cite shared custody. Is this correct?'

'Yes, but—'

'And is it not true that *equal* and *share*, in legal terminology, do not have the same meaning?'

A faint frown creased the lawyer's forehead. 'Not precisely.'

'In which case, it could be argued as a literal interpretation?' Dante sensed the sudden stillness in Taylor's body language.

'Where are you going with this?'

He shifted his attention and caught the edge of suspicion sharpening her eyes. 'We've explored the available options, and failed to agree on any one of them.' He didn't give her time to offer so much as a word as he pursued, 'I propose we share custody of Ben in the same home. This way he will have the best of care and we will both be a constant in his life.'

Taylor's lips parted, then closed again. 'That's the most ridiculous suggestion I've ever heard,' she said shakily. 'Even if it were viable, my apartment is too small to accommodate you.'

His mouth curved into a faint smile, and was totally at variance with the stillness evident in his dark, almost black eyes.

'As it happens I have a property available for

immediate occupancy at Watson's Bay,' he continued as if she hadn't spoken. 'It's a double-storeyed residence with seven bedrooms situated on an upper level divided into two separate wings. Two individual offices, a home gym, indoor pool. There's also separate accommodation for a live-in housekeeper.' He spared her a conciliatory look. 'Sharing the same house shouldn't prove too difficult. You'll have primary care of Ben when I'm overseas on business, and from your perspective very little will change.'

You *think*? She could only look at him in a state of speechlessness.

'It negates each of your objections,' Dante informed silkily. 'Ben remains in Sydney in your care for seventy-five per cent of the time, with all of the advantages I'm able to provide.'

The lawyer shifted his attention to Taylor. 'Mr d'Alessandri's suggestion is exceedingly generous.'

Why did she have the unshakable feeling she'd been very cleverly manipulated by a master strategist?

Taylor cast Dante a dazed look, torn by

numerous emotions, none of which resembled *calm*. 'I'll need to think about it.'

She turned to the lawyer, thanked him, then she stood and moved towards the door.

Dante reached it before she did, and she was powerless to prevent the feathery sensation scudding down her spine as he accompanied her to the bank of lifts.

'I'd like to see my nephew as soon as possible.'

She'd expected the request. 'Ben is in kindergarten today,' she relayed evenly.

'From where you're due to collect him *when*?'

'Three o'clock,' Taylor revealed with deceptive calm.

The lift arrived and she was supremely conscious of his presence in the confined space. Her eyes were level with the generous curve of his mouth, and the faint exclusive tones of his cologne teased her senses.

She'd felt relaxed in Leon's presence, whereas Dante exuded a brooding sensuality that had always threatened her peace of mind.

Like you *care*? a tiny voice prompted. You have every reason to distrust men, remember?

A tiny shiver slid down her spine. As if she could ever forget.

She didn't recall holding her breath during the lift's descent, although she must have done so unconsciously, for she measured its release as she stepped into the foyer.

'Have you eaten?'

The question came out of left field, and she looked at him in startled surprise. 'Why do you ask?'

'We need to formulate arrangements regarding Ben's welfare.'

She opened her mouth to protest, only to have him continue smoothly, 'Why not share a meal while we do so?'

'It doesn't have to encompass lunch.'

Dante paused as they reached the pavement. 'You'd prefer we adjourn to your apartment?'

No. The negation was a silent scream inside her head, and it took a few seemingly long seconds to summon her voice to project a polite veneer. 'There are a few cafés close by,' she acquiesced evenly, and missed the slight hardening in his eyes. 'Perhaps a sandwich and coffee?'

He led her to a restaurant, and ignored her protest as the *maître d'* seated them.

'I dislike—'

'Not having total control?' Dante intercepted with deceptive mildness, and caught the way her eyes flared green.

'It's something at which you appear to excel,' Taylor said, tongue firmly in cheek.

He accepted the wine list, and requested her preference.

'Iced water is fine.' Her tolerance level was diminishing by the second. Any minute soon she'd be tempted to toss the contents of her glass in his face.

'I wouldn't advise it,' he said quietly, as if again reading her mind, and speared her with a look that promised retribution.

She collected her bag and stood, only to stifle an audible gasp as his hand closed over her wrist.

'Sit. Please,' he added.

She glared at him. 'Give me one reason why I should.'

'Ben.'

The little boy's image filled her mind, his

solemn saddened eyes…and knew she'd give anything to provide a happy, healthy life for him. 'It will never work.'

'Lunch?'

Taylor gave him an exasperated look. 'Sharing the same house.'

'As far as Ben is concerned, given all your reasons, it's the best option.'

She opened her mouth, then closed it again as the waiter appeared to take their order.

Dammit, she hadn't even looked at the menu, let alone made a selection.

'Taylor?'

She met the silent challenge in his gaze, hesitated, then ordered a Caesar salad, and waited until they were alone before venturing, 'You employ unfair tactics.' She lifted the goblet of iced water, took a sip, then carefully replaced it.

To his credit he didn't attempt to misunderstand. 'Had it been my initial suggestion, you would have immediately dismissed it out of hand.'

'I have yet to agree,' she ventured, and held his measured look.

'Common sense ensures you will.'

Her eyes sharpened. 'And if I don't?'

Dante took his time before answering, 'Then you leave me no option but to lodge an application to formally adopt Ben.'

CHAPTER TWO

SHOCK dilated Taylor's eyes, and she felt the blood drain from her face.

'You can't do that,' she managed shakily. 'Such an action would contravene Leon and Casey's will.'

Dante's features held a compelling quality, and a chill shiver feathered the length of her spine.

'Leon's lawyer is witness to you declining each solution I presented.' His voice held a silky softness that was totally lacking in arrogance, yet there was a dangerous quality evident beneath the surface. 'Unless you choose to reverse your decision, you leave me little option but to take the matter to court.'

She didn't trust herself to speak. At the very least she wanted to hit him, and if a mere look could kill he'd be dead.

'Such a move would involve time and a large amount of money,' Dante enlightened smoothly.

She owned her apartment, her car, and was debt-free, thanks to the popularity of her work. But when it came to wealth, Dante d'Alessandri won hands down.

'Do you particularly want to go that route?' he pursued silkily. 'Subject Ben to unwarranted stress and trauma? Fund exhaustive legal fees?' He waited a beat. 'What will it achieve, other than an exercise in futility?'

'Except at the end of the day you win.' She attempted to keep the faint bitterness out of her voice, and was unsure she succeeded.

His eyes remained steady, inviolate. 'This is about Ben,' he reminded quietly. 'And what's best for him.'

It didn't help that he was right. Or that she viewed his threatened alternative of adoption as totally unconscionable.

There was no way she'd allow that to happen, although she refused to give in easily without protest.

The waiter delivered their meal, and Taylor

looked at the salad, contemplated her plate and wondered if she'd be able to eat so much as a morsel.

'I don't want to share a house with you.' And if you comment I'm the first woman to say that, I'll *hit* you.

He looked at her carefully, caught the fast-beating pulse at the base of her throat, and his eyes narrowed fractionally.

'There's a boyfriend on the scene who will object?'

A fleeting darkness clouded her eyes, then it was gone. 'No.' Betrayed trust ensured true friends were limited to a few, and acquaintances kept at a distance.

Interpreting body language and subtle nuances in the human voice was an art in which he excelled…an invaluable asset in the cut and thrust of international business dealings.

It took, Dante mused, an accomplished actress trained to submerge her own personality in order to assume that of the character she was con-tracted to play.

And somehow he doubted Taylor was playing

a part. Yet he'd stake his reputation on there being something responsible for her chosen façade...even allowing for recent grief, and Ben's welfare.

'And you, Dante? Won't your current mistress protest at your proposed live-in arrangement with another woman?'

'No.'

Just...*no*?

'Eat,' Dante bade and he began doing justice to the food on his plate.

The salad looked delicious...although her nerves were stretched too taut to appreciate the taste of food.

She declined dessert and settled for coffee, sweet, black and strong, aware it was also Dante's choice, and when the waiter presented the bill she reached for her wallet...only to have Dante refuse her offer to pay her share.

'There's enough time to check out the house before we collect Ben.'

House? *We?* 'I don't think—'

'We have an hour and a half,' he enlightened as he ushered her out onto the pavement. All it took was a brief conversation via his mobile phone, and within minutes a black Mercedes slid in to the kerb.

Dante opened a door, ushered her into the rear seat, then he crossed round the vehicle and slipped in beside her, introduced his driver, Gianni, with friendly ease. Given Dante's reputed ruthlessness in the business arena, she assumed he'd appear businesslike with his staff, and she sat in silence as he issued instructions to an address in Watson's Bay, one of Sydney's luxurious suburbs offering widespread panoramic harbour views.

House was a misnomer. *Mansion* seemed a more adequate description, Taylor conceded as the Mercedes swept through high, ornate remotely operated steel gates, circled a wide driveway and eased to a halt beneath a wide *porte-cochère* protecting broad double entrance doors of steel-strutted solid patterned wood.

Double-storeyed, the building resembled a Tuscan villa, with a cream and terra-cotta tiled roof, cream stucco exterior walls and, she saw when she entered the large lobby, cream marble floor tiles, beautiful rugs and solid mahogany furniture.

A middle-aged woman came forward to greet them. Dante introduced her as Anna, whose husband, Claude, maintained the grounds.

There were oil paintings gracing the walls, an elegant, sweeping double staircase, and a sparkling crystal chandelier hung suspended from a tall ceiling.

Taylor was supremely conscious of Dante's close proximity as he showed her through the house.

The subtle tones of his cologne teased her senses, and, although he made no attempt at physical contact, she disliked the prickle of awareness stealing through her body.

She covered it well, making appropriate comments as they moved through the ground-level rooms, all of which were spacious, beautifully furnished, before moving to the upper level, which did, as Dante had indicated, contain two distinct wings, each containing guest suites with adjoining *en suites*. There was also a media room, a family lounge and two home offices.

It was, Taylor had to concede, a beautiful

home, complemented by landscaped grounds, a large swimming pool with entry from the side of the house and completely enclosed with a solar-tinted glass roof and glass-panelled external walls.

There was no valid reason why Dante's suggested living arrangement couldn't work...with certain iron-clad provisos.

'Any reservations you'd care to voice?' Dante queried as they began descending the staircase, and she met his dark, probing look with equanimity.

'A few.'

'Then let's hear them.'

She paused on one step and turned towards him, aware he copied her action.

'I want to make it very clear Ben is the only reason I'll accept your suggestion.'

'So noted.'

'The live-in arrangement is strictly business,' she offered, and lifted a hand to cover the telltale thud at the base of her throat, 'with all that statement implies.'

Dante looked at her for a long moment, aware

she held his gaze with determined resolve, almost silently daring him to be the first to glance away.

Yet beneath the resolve he sensed unaccustomed wariness and a degree of fragility. Coupled with innate reserve, it was an interesting mix.

'You have nothing to fear from me,' he drawled, and saw a delicate pink tinge her cheeks an instant before she turned away and began stepping quickly down the stairs.

Dante checked his watch, alerted Gianni, then he followed Taylor down into the lobby and led the way to the waiting Mercedes.

It was a relatively trouble-free run from Vaucluse to Double Bay, and Dante turned slightly towards her as the car slid into a parking bay adjacent the kindergarten. 'I'll come with you.'

She could hardly refuse without sounding churlish, and she managed a polite response. 'Ben will be pleased to see you.'

Dante's presence drew attention as they crossed towards the kindergarten entrance, his tall, broad, impeccably tailored frame a stand-out from the few males gathered waiting to collect children.

Within minutes the outer door opened, and a

carer took up position to ensure each child was collected by their designated parent or grandparent.

Taylor effected an introduction, drew attention
to the fact she'd previously noted Dante as Ben's
legal guardian, whereupon relevant details were
checked on the call-sheet, together with Dante's
mobile-phone number.

'Please alter the residential address,' Dante
informed, and gave it. 'Effective from today,' he
added smoothly.

Excuse me?

'Isn't this a little precipitate?' she said quietly
as they moved aside, and incurred his dark gaze.

'There's no reason to delay settling Ben into
his new home.'

Taylor sent him a spearing look. 'Tomorrow,'
she stated firmly. 'It will allow him to become accustomed to the idea.'

Minutes later Ben was summoned by the carer,
whereupon he moved quickly to the entrance,
leant into her hug, then a smile broadened his
mouth as he caught sight of Dante.

Without a word he raised his arms as Dante lifted
him high against his chest and held him close.

'Hello, Ben.'

'Zio. You came. Taylor said you would.' Ben looked at him solemnly. 'Are you going to stay?'

'Yes. Most of the time,' Dante assured as he crossed the parking area.

'Cool.'

One word, conveying much, and Taylor felt her heart melt a little...as it had so often these past few weeks, when all she wanted to do was hug him close and will back his laughter and joy of life.

Time. It will just take time, she assured silently as they reached the Mercedes, and she frowned with sudden anxiety. 'Ben's booster seat is in my car.'

Dante spared her a glance. 'I had Gianni organise one this morning.' He opened the rear door, saw Ben safely buckled in as she slid in beside her nephew, while Dante took the adjacent seat.

She knew she should credit Dante with forethought, but he was moving too fast, taking control...doubtless a power trait he'd skilfully honed as head of the d'Alessandri corporation.

Laudable, but Ben wasn't a corporate commodity, and she intended to relay her viewpoint at the soonest possible moment.

A strange prickling sensation at the back of her neck caused her to spare a glance in Dante's direction, and the breath stopped in her throat as she met his musing gaze.

He couldn't possibly know what she was thinking, surely? Oh, for heaven's sake…it hardly mattered if he *did*.

Taylor offered Gianni directions to her apartment, and she felt a sense of relief when the car slid to a halt at the kerb outside what had once been a stately double-storeyed villa which developers had converted into four apartments.

'Thanks for lunch,' she acknowledged quietly as Dante withdrew Ben and set him onto his feet on the pavement.

Ben's hand curled into his uncle's much larger one as he looked up at her. 'Can Zio come up and see my bike?'

How could she refuse? 'Of course. If he'd like to.' She almost qualified it with 'if he isn't too busy', and stilled the words before they could find voice.

Did Dante sense her reluctance? Perhaps, although she told herself his thought process was of little interest.

Her apartment was one of two situated on the upper floor, reached by a wide central staircase, and she unlocked the door, disarmed the alarm system, then indicated the hallway. 'Would you like coffee?'

'Thanks, that would be nice.' He smiled down at Ben's anxious features. 'Let's go see your bike, shall we?'

The apartment was relatively spacious and pleasantly furnished. Two bedrooms, two bathrooms, the usual utilities. Feminine, but functional, he noted as Ben led him into a room where floor-to-ceiling bookcases lined two walls. A home office, *sans* a desk, computer or the usual electronic equipment.

Instead stuffed toys lined the bed, and there were several toy cars and trucks neatly parked together on the floor. A few childish prints were attached to the wall above the bed, together with an enlarged framed photo taken in happier times featuring Casey, Leon, Ben as a young babe and Taylor.

Dante's gaze lingered, settled briefly on Taylor's features, noting her happy smile, the laughing eyes…as if she hadn't a care in the world.

'This is my bike.'

Dante hunkered down and ran a careful hand over the gleaming paint, the seat, and commented on its racy three-wheeler design.

'Daddy bought it for me, before—' He paused, bit his lip, then reiterated with extreme care, 'Before.'

Dante suddenly felt a fierce need to draw Ben close and assure him everything would be fine. Instead, he rubbed a gentle palm over Ben's shoulder, kept it there for a moment, then offered warmly, 'Maybe we can take it to a park one day soon and you can show me how well you can ride.'

Dark brown eyes regarded him solemnly. 'Can Taylor come too?'

'Of course.'

A tentative smile widened his mouth. 'Are you going to stay with us?'

'Would you like that?'

'You can have my bed.'

Such an earnest offer, and one that pulled at

something deep within. This was Leon's son, *his* godson. A child who needed every reassurance he was safe, secure and loved.

'That's very kind,' Dante said gently. 'Perhaps we should run it by Taylor?' It would allow her the opportunity to reveal their imminent move to Watson's Bay.

Which it did, and he silently applauded her explanation, added his own together with the benefits of sharing a larger residence.

They kept it simple, logical...and received Ben's slow nod of acceptance, pursued by a worried frown. 'Will I still go to the same kindergarten?'

In a time of complete change, it was important to retain a constant. 'Yes.' Dante's assurance echoed that of Taylor's, and Ben's expression cleared.

'And can Sooty come, too?'

Dante raised an eyebrow in silent query, and Taylor quickly explained, 'Sooty is a cat.'

'Of course.'

Taylor opted for informality, choosing to serve coffee at the dining-room table, where Ben sat enjoying his glass of milk and afternoon snack.

Dante's presence had an unsettling effect… one she endeavoured to overcome as she focused on Ben, waiting for the moment Dante would leave.

Except he seemed in no hurry, and she felt her nerves stretch increasingly taut.

Almost as if he knew, he made a play of checking his watch. 'If you'll excuse me?'

She caught the faint gleam of amusement as he rose to his feet, and for a brief moment her eyes flared in silent response as he placed a hand on Ben's shoulder.

'I'll see you tomorrow.'

'And Taylor.'

Dante's smile held affection. 'Yes. Taylor, too.'

It wasn't difficult to summon a degree of warmth as she preceded him to the door, and she determinedly held his gaze for the few seemingly long seconds before he passed into the small lobby and descended the stairs to the main entrance.

There was a sense of relief as she secured the lock, then she summoned Ben for his routine of bath followed by dinner. Then she read him a bedtime story…extended by a host of inevitable questions which she managed to answer with the assurance he needed.

It was only later as Ben slept that she contemplated her own need for reassurance.

As from tomorrow she'd be living with an inimitable man and, despite the large house, there would be far more togetherness than she felt comfortable with.

So get used to it.

At least on one issue they each stood firm… taking care of Ben. That had to be a *good* thing.

Dante made it sound so…simple. A large mansion, separate living wings, he'd be overseas more often than he'd be at home.

Why, they'd probably rarely see each other!

CHAPTER THREE

ATTENDING to the packing of both Ben's and her own belongings involved more than simply transferring a number of boxes in one car. She needed her reference and research books for her current work in progress, laptop, printer, fax, as well as several notebooks, disks.

Then there were personal items, such as her and Ben's clothing. It was just as well Dante had offered Claude's services and a four-wheel drive, for it took three trips before Taylor closed up and secured her apartment, then followed Claude in her Lexus.

It was way too late to have second thoughts as she entered Dante's mansion and attempted to accept this was now her home for the fore-seeable future.

The home itself didn't faze her…but its owner

did. A telling admission, and one she tried hard to dismiss. Without success.

For the umpteenth time she wondered at her sanity, only to once again temporarily banish her reservations by reaffirming the sharing of Dante's home was the best option for Ben.

And the best for Ben was what Casey would have wanted.

Taylor offered Claude a genuine smile and thanked him for his help as she followed him upstairs, where Anna, bless her, had supervised the boxes into each guest suite.

Together they completed Ben's suite, involving him in the process by suggesting he display his toys, before setting up her home office. Lastly, her own suite, which she assured she'd tend to herself.

All told, the moving and unpacking process took most of the day, and there was time for a quick shower, a change of clothes before she readied Ben for dinner.

Please let it just be the two of us, Taylor bade silently as she took Ben's hand and they made their way downstairs to the dining room. The thought of sharing a meal and conversation with Dante accelerated her nervous tension a few levels, and she offered up a silent appeal to the deity both she and Ben might eat alone.

Except the appeal went unanswered, for Dante was there as they entered the room, standing tall, without his usual attire of jacket and tie, his shirt-sleeves rolled to halfway on his forearms, an easy smile softening the hard planes of his face as he moved forward with the grace of a jungle cat.

'I believe you've settled in?' The query was directed to include both of them, and Taylor inclined her head, while Ben offered solemnly,

'We put all my toys out. And Taylor's room is close to mine. Sooty has her bed and kitty litter in my bathroom.'

She watched as Dante lifted Ben and rested him into the crook of his arm.

'Sooty stays with me at night.' Ben spared Dante an anxious look. 'Taylor lets her sleep on my bed.'

Please don't say no, Taylor begged silently.

'I used to have a cat who slept on my bed when I was young,' Dante confided, and Ben's eyes widened.

'You did? What colour was your cat? Sooty's black. She has a white patch on her nose.'

'I had Baci, a tortoiseshell.'

'Baci means kisses,' Ben relayed importantly, and Dante smiled in acknowledgment.

'Yes, it does.'

An innocuous remark, Taylor conceded...so why did it suddenly send awareness spiralling through her body?

Because she was tired, fraught and feeling way out of her depth. *Why*, she agonised silently, when she had nothing to fear from the man whose home she occupied?

A good night's sleep was all she needed. A day or two to accept concrete evidence of her new reality.

At that moment Anna appeared bearing a tray containing a steaming casserole and a dish of rice, together with a platter of assorted vegetables.

Taylor took the chair Dante indicated and seated Ben next to her, while he took the chair opposite.

Did he sense her nervousness? She hoped not. Yet she found it impossible to relax, and she ate mechanically. At the end of the meal she selected fresh fruit in lieu of dessert, and requested tea instead of coffee.

In a way it was a relief when the meal concluded, and Ben provided the perfect reason to escape.

'Can I please go upstairs and check Sooty? I think she might be lonely.'

'Of course. I'll come with you,' Taylor said quickly, and caught the faint amusement evident in Dante's dark gaze.

'Perhaps we could go together,' he suggested. 'You can show me your toys.'

Ben didn't hesitate, and for the ensuing hour man and boy communed on the merits of almost every wheeled vehicle currently on offer...including planes, trains and automobiles. For so young a boy, Ben could reel off a number of brand names...his favourite being a red Ferrari. Something he fervently hoped to own one day. Together with a motorbike.

Every boy's dream, and he happily didn't protest when she declared it was time for bed.

'Taylor reads me a story every night.' He looked at his uncle. 'Will you stay and read me one, too? Please, Zio Dante.'

'Of course, if you'd like me to.'

Something Dante appeared only too willing to do…whenever he was home, she added silently, which hopefully wouldn't be too often.

A prediction which didn't hold true, for he shared breakfast with them the next morning, and sat down to dinner each evening. Ben's bedtime story became a nightly event, and Friday evening Dante added to Ben's wish-list by suggesting they visit a dog breeder at the weekend in order to choose a puppy.

Not, praise heaven, Taylor begged silently, something with the potential to grow too big.

'A Llasa Apso,' Dante revealed, sparing her a musing glance.

Did he read minds? Or were her thoughts merely too easy to interpret?

'They're a small breed, and in this instance they're already trained.' He reached into his shirt pocket, withdrew a folded coloured print and showed it to Ben. 'What do you think?'

Taylor saw Ben's expression change into instant love, and the look he cast Dante held a degree of reverent awe. 'Can I really have one?'

'Yes, and we can bring it home.'

'You're the best.' Ben's eyes shone as he lifted his arms and gave Dante a hug. 'Thank you.'

Dante returned the embrace and brushed his lips to his nephew's forehead. 'Time to go to sleep, hmm? Tomorrow will be a big day.'

Dante stood aside as Taylor tucked in the covers and kissed Ben goodnight before preceding Dante from the room.

'That's kind of you,' she said quietly. 'Leon had promised Ben a puppy for his birthday.'

He indicated the stairs and they began descending to the lower floor.

'You think I'm attempting to buy Ben's affection?'

She shot him a startled look. 'A puppy is a perfect gift. Casey didn't feel Ben should grow up thinking he could have anything he wants.'

He indicated the library, followed her in, then gestured towards a comfortable leather chair.

'I fly out to New York on Monday for a few days, possibly longer,' he revealed as he crossed to lean a hip against the antique desk. 'You can contact me via my cellphone. You have the number.'

'I'm sure it won't be necessary.'

No, it probably wouldn't. She was efficient, capable and considered Ben her main priority.

He slanted an eyebrow and his mouth curved in to form a light smile. 'You could always call and say *hello*.'

'I wouldn't think of disturbing you.'

Did she have any idea the pulse at the base of her throat quickened in beat whenever she was in his presence?

Her controlled persona was a façade...and he wondered what lay beneath it.

He'd given her no reason to be wary of him, yet she wasn't comfortable...and he was sufficiently intrigued to discover why.

In time.

'I'll set up a computer here, with a web-cam. It'll enable Ben to have daily visual contact with me.'

He had the sudden urge to ruffle her composure, see those beautiful eyes dilate and watch the pulse at the base of her throat thud into a quickened beat.

Her reaction intrigued him...as she did. So outwardly practical. Laudable, but it was what lay beneath that held his interest. Had done so for quite some time. Yet distance and the pressure of business worked against him. Now, given unforeseen circumstance, he had all the time in the world.

'If that's all you wanted,' Taylor offered as she rose to her feet, 'I'll say goodnight…and thank you.'

His eyes became faintly hooded, and a slow smile curved his generous mouth. 'Thank me for what, precisely?'

'Making the effort to ensure the transition is as easy as possible for Ben.'

He inclined his head. 'And you, Taylor?' he pursued softly. 'Has the transition into my home, my life, been easy for you?'

No. She wanted to say he had to know that, for it disturbed her how well he appeared to read her.

'I'm sure the arrangement will work out well,' she concurred politely. With that, she moved to the door, opened it and escaped into the wide hallway, uncaring whether Dante followed or not.

The acquisition of a puppy proved a huge success, together with kennel, puppy toys, bowls and various trappings a well-cared-for puppy should have. Rosie, for the Llasa Apso Ben chose was female, lapped up all the loving attention Ben offered, and returned it in kind. Dante's absence in New York provided Taylor with a welcome break from his presence, although his image was *there* every evening at a prearranged time via the computer web-cam as he chatted to Ben.

Taylor was careful to keep her conversation to a minimum, offering a polite greeting on connection, followed by an equally polite 'goodnight' prior to deactivating the web-cam.

Did he guess at her apparent reluctance to participate in more than a perfunctory sentence or two? Undoubtedly. For she glimpsed the slight curve at the edge of his mouth, the faint musing gleam in his dark eyes.

It was Ben who relayed a birthday invitation for Sunday.

'My friend Tamryn is having a party because she is going to be four. Taylor is taking me, and I wondered if you could come, too. Please, Zio. Will you be home in time?'

'I'll do my best,' Dante assured. 'Taylor can give me the details tomorrow evening.'

'Cool.'

Sunday provided sunshine and crisp temperatures, and Ben's excitement was engaging as the time to leave for the party drew close.

'Everyone from kindy is going to be at Tamryn's house.'

Taylor dropped a kiss on the top of his head. 'You'll have lots of fun.'

His eyes shone with anticipation. 'Tamryn says there's going to be a clown, and rides, and a huge big rubber house to play in.' He barely paused for breath. 'Can we go now?'

'Sure we can.' She picked up the brightly wrapped present with its fun card. 'Shall we say goodbye to Anna first?'

'And Claude,' Ben added. 'He's in the garden.'

It didn't take long, and the adherence to good manners brought forth a smile as both Anna and her husband bade Ben goodbye and hoped he enjoyed the party.

The invitation stated two o'clock, and Taylor drew the car into the kerb outside a large, stately home in suburban Woollahra.

A security guard manned the gate, checking invitations as guests arrived and offering directions to the rear of the grounds, where the party was set up.

'There's Tamryn.'

Taylor felt the sudden tightening of Ben's hand within her own, and she gave his a reassuring squeeze as they drew close to a group of excited children all dressed in their finest, and mingling parents.

'You're going to stay, aren't you?'

'Hey,' she chided gently, 'you think I'm going to miss out on all the fun?'

And it *was* fun; the professional planning ensured there was spontaneity in the children's games, with thirty-odd pre-schoolers enjoying the time of their lives. Any minor squabble was intercepted, the perpetrator distracted, and eventually it was time for food, drink...and most importantly, the cake.

It was easy to smile, to laugh a little at so many small faces glowing with anticipation as four candles were ceremoniously lit.

A sudden prickle of awareness slid up Taylor's spine and settled at her nape...an instinctive alert she endeavoured to ignore without much success.

She shifted her gaze slightly and caught sight of the tall, broad-shouldered male figure crossing the grounds towards the host, hostess and their grouped guests.

Dante. Attired in dark tailored trousers, a white shirt open at the neck, worn with a black butter-soft leather jacket.

It wasn't so much his attire that drew attention but the man himself, for there was an intrinsic quality she chose not to define…just aware of an instinctive need to build her defensive barriers high in self-protection.

Survival…her own. Against a man whose sensual potency threatened to wreck her equilibrium. Something she vowed no man would ever be permitted to do again.

Why *now*, when she'd reached a relatively relaxed state of mind? Settled, she added silently, into a life of relative contentment.

Yet in one fatal second her world had changed, flung into an orbit she struggled to control.

Not Ben…never Ben.

Dante.

A man who disturbed her more than she was prepared to admit. Had from the moment she first saw him. Friendly, warm…with a reputation for preferring sophisticated women who knew the score.

It wasn't her nature to flirt. Nor did she favour casual sex, possibly because there had been no one for whom she'd been tempted to discard her moral beliefs.

Besides, Dante resided abroad and travelled the world. Any liaison with such a man could only be destined for heartbreak…and she was fiercely determined it wouldn't be *hers*.

Later she had reason to enforce that decision a hundredfold.

Yet now he was in her life, occupying her mind, infiltrating her senses, and she struggled against it…wanting only the tranquil life that had once been her own.

'Taylor.'

She turned slightly and tilted her face a little to meet his easy smile. He had the advantage of height, marked by her choice of flat shoes for the afternoon.

'Hi.'

There was strength apparent beneath the casual elegance of his clothes. A compelling quality that stood him apart from other men. *Power*, she determined, and an innate sense of control. Mesh it with latent sexuality, and the result drew women's attention like bees to a honeypot.

Hadn't she witnessed evidence of it at every opportunity?

'Ben will be pleased you managed to make it.'

The sparkling laughter he'd glimpsed had faded, replaced by polite friendliness...and he resisted the temptation to cup her cheek, smooth a thumb over her lips, feel them tremble a little beneath his touch.

Almost as if she sensed his intention, her body stiffened, and the edge of his mouth lifted a little with the knowledge she was aware of the electric tension existing between them.

'I wouldn't disappoint him.' His voice was a silken drawl as his gaze lingered briefly on the pulsing beat at the edge of her throat, then shifted to acknowledge Ben's excited wave. 'It's good to see he's enjoying himself.'

'Yes.'

Ben raced towards them, arms outstretched as he reached his uncle, and Taylor watched as Dante lifted him high against his chest to settle him in the crook of one arm.

'We're all getting a present,' Ben enlightened with excitement. 'And Tamryn says the party isn't over yet.' He transferred an anxious look from his uncle to Taylor. 'We can stay, can't we?'

'Of course,' Dante conceded easily.

It became a pleasant hour as the parents mixed and mingled while the children were supervised at play.

Drinks were offered, together with coffee, tea and canapés...and fairy lights illuminated the grounds as the sun faded beyond the horizon.

Dante rarely moved from Taylor's side, projecting a unified front...one she chose to dissemble without much success.

It was almost seven when they collected Ben, bade Tamryn goodnight and thanked the little girl's parents for the party invitation.

Ben was already beginning to droop as Dante hoisted him high onto his shoulders and accompanied Taylor out to the car.

It had been an exciting day for a little boy, who once they reached home, wanted only a glass of milk after his bath, and fell asleep almost as soon as his head touched the pillow.

'Anna has prepared dinner,' Dante relayed as they quietly closed Ben's door behind them.

Togetherness was a fine thing, but Taylor was in overload, and a little wired from spending a few hours in his company.

'I'm really not hungry.'

A statement which incurred an intense look. 'You barely ate a thing at the party.'

'I'm fine.' He saw too much, divined more, and it put her on edge. 'I'll grab a banana, coffee, and spend time on my laptop.'

'I'll have Anna bring you a tray.'

She raged a silent battle for a few seconds, then ventured with extreme politeness, 'I'm capable of doing that myself.'

Dark eyes speared her own, and held, almost

as if he *knew*, then he inclined his head. 'Your prerogative.'

'Thank you.'

The air seemed to hold a curious tension...something she chose to ignore as she descended the stairs and made her way to the kitchen, where she apologised to Anna for her lack of appetite, then with a mug of fresh coffee in one hand, a banana in the other, she bade Dante and Anna 'goodnight'.

'Don't work too late.'

Taylor sensed mild amusement beneath his indolent voice, and told herself she didn't care if he thought she was avoiding him.

What was more, she'd work as late as she liked.

She occupied his home, but she was damned if he'd tell her what to do!

Consequently she entered the home office, opened her laptop, reread the previous day's work and wrote...weaving characters, motive and suspense into script, becoming lost in the fascination of creative process.

Occasionally she rose from the chair, flexed her shoulders and executed a few calisthenics to ease the tension of repetitive movement.

The night hours were her most productive writing time, and when she'd lived in her apartment she'd often lost track of time, realising the lateness of the hour only when her eyes began to blur…

Now, however, she no longer lived alone… there was Ben, and the compelling man whose home she shared.

Dante, who had led her to believe they'd rarely see each other…except he was *there*, at every opportunity sharing her life and becoming a large, fundamental part of Ben's.

So why did it bother her so much? Taylor attempted to rationalise on the edge of sleep…and failed to discover a sensible answer.

CHAPTER FOUR

TAYLOR watched as Dante swept Ben high against his chest as he prepared to leave for the airport...heard the young boy's delighted laughter, and felt a pang of envy for the easy affection they shared.

It brought so vividly alive how much she missed Casey...the frequent phone calls, *sharing*, the unconditional affection and innate knowledge they were always *there* for each other.

A huge gap she attempted to bridge with love for her nephew.

It was enough, she assured fiercely...all she needed. Her writing career was an added bonus and the success it had brought her ensured she was busy and her mind occupied for much of the time too.

So why the longing for something *more*?

The touch of a man's lips on her own. Strong, warm arms enfolding her close. Affection. Trust.

The knowledge that she was safe.

'When will you be back?'

Her voice sounded slightly uneven, and she caught the sudden sharpness in Dante's eyes, then it was gone.

'A week, perhaps less.'

Taylor summoned a smile as he released Ben down onto his feet. 'Take care.' The words seemed fairly innocuous as she caught her nephew's hand and crossed the lobby at Dante's side.

Gianni was seated behind the wheel of the Mercedes as Dante released one of the large doors and moved lithely down the few steps to slide into the front passenger seat.

Ben waved until the car swept through the electronic gates and disappeared from sight.

'I wish Zio didn't have to go away.'

She drew him close and dropped a kiss on his nose. Poor little scrap, he sounded quite forlorn.

'He's a very busy man,' she offered gently, and met solemn dark eyes.

'He promised he'll call tonight before I go to bed.'

One thing she'd learnt was that Dante kept to his word. 'I'm sure he will.' She caught hold of his hand and bestowed a teasing smile. 'Now, young man, let's go have breakfast.'

After which she'd oversee his normal morning routine, help him dress, pack his knapsack, drive him to kindergarten…then she'd return to seek seclusion in her home office and write until it was time to go collect Ben.

It was a plan which should work reasonably well, if she managed to gain total focus on the twist needed to extend the suspense element in the story she was currently working on.

The ability to clear her mind and enter the fictional world of her characters required concentrated effort, and fortified with a cup of Earl Grey tea, she opened her current manuscript file and reread the previous day's work, edited and made a few minor changes before tuning in to the creative process.

At midday she took a break and fixed herself a ham and salad sandwich in the kitchen, filled a glass with apple juice and chose to eat lunch on the terrace.

The sun held little warmth and there was a fresh breeze which hinted at late afternoon showers, borne by a bank of clouds hovering on the horizon.

There were days when she permitted her mind to wander during a lunch break...others when she preferred to keep the momentum going by printing out the morning's hard copy and editing it as she ate.

Today there was a tendency to lapse into introspection and enjoy the sensation of freedom from Dante's presence for several days.

Leading separate lives whilst residing beneath the same roof wasn't really happening, Taylor reflected.

Whether by accident or design Dante entered the informal dining room and shared breakfast with her and Ben each morning...and most evenings he arrived home from the city office in time to join them for dinner. What was more, he supervised Ben's bath-time, and shared the telling of their nephew's bedtime story.

Whatever her reservations, she had to concede Dante had Ben's continuing welfare at heart as he displayed genuine caring and affection at every turn.

Gradually Ben's tendency towards solemnity was beginning to fade as he smiled more often, and the occasional bad dreams where he woke crying in the night were beginning to diminish.

The move into Dante's home was proving to be the right choice...for Ben.

So why was she so tense and on edge? Instinctively wary and unable to relax?

The simmering electricity existent beneath the surface whenever she was in Dante's presence... what was that?

Did he sense it? Or was it merely a figment of her imagination?

Whatever, it was a complication she didn't want or need.

Oh, for heaven's sake...*take a reality check*, why don't you?

She was one of two surrogate parents, committed to raising their nephew together. This was all about Ben...*all of it.*

She shared a beautiful, spacious house with a home office to die for, her own suite of rooms, staff to cook and clean, financial freedom.

So why did she have this niggling feeling something was missing? It hardly made sense.

Taylor drained the rest of her juice from her glass, collected her plate and returned both to the kitchen, then she filched a bottle of water from the refrigerator and retreated back to her work until it was time to collect Ben from kindergarten.

He burst through the door when summoned, a finger-painting clutched in one hand, his knapsack in the other, and a delighted smile lighting his face.

'I got a gold star!'

She caught him close in a warm hug. 'You did? That's fantastic.'

'I did a finger-painting of you, me and Zio Dante. Shelley said it's very good.'

Shelley was one of the carers employed to teach and supervise the pupils…a young, bubbly brunette adored by the children.

'Can I see it?'

Ben unfolded the paper with care and took

great pride in identifying each figure. 'That's you with long hair, and I made Dante big, 'cos he's tall, and that's me.'

Taylor felt her heartstrings tug a little at the sight of a small figure holding the hand of the adult standing either side of him.

Her eyes welled with moisture, and she swept him into her arms. 'It's a beautiful painting.'

Ben looked at her closely. 'Why are you crying?'

'Because I love you so much.'

'Me, too.'

She unashamedly wiped her eyes, then she carried him to the car, secured him in the rear seat, then brushed her lips to his cheek.

'Would you like to go to the park?'

His eyes widened. 'Did you bring my bike?'

'It's in the boot.'

'Cool.'

He ate the banana she'd brought for him and drank some of the bottled water when they reached the park, then she unloaded his bike.

They spent a lovely hour together as he rode his bike along the winding pathways, and afterwards he entered the playground, where he took turns on the swing, enjoyed the jungle-gym, then spent time climbing the steps to the slide.

There were other young children playing with a football, and he joined them for a while before happily riding his bike towards the car.

It was almost five when they arrived home, and with due ceremony the finger-painting was pinned onto a cork-board on Ben's bedroom wall.

Dinner was served at six, followed a while later by his bath-time, then at the pre-arranged time of seven-fifteen Taylor logged on to her computer, settled Ben close, engaged the web-cam and watched as Dante's features filled the screen.

Close, much too close. So much so, she felt if she reached out she could touch him.

Yet he was such a long way away…checking in as he'd said he would, so that his presence seemed a constant in a vulnerable young boy's life.

So why did it seem as if he were in the same room, his dark eyes lazily appreciative as he listened to Ben excitedly relaying an afternoon sojourn at a park?

And why, when Dante switched his attention

to her, did her body quiver a little, and the pulse at the base of her throat beat a fast tattoo?

There was the temptation to lift fingers to cover her body's visible betrayal, except such a gesture would highlight rather than hide her reaction.

Instead, she managed a credible smile, assured all was well and wondered, not for the first time, why Dante left her feeling as if she was being caught up in a whirlwind.

It wasn't any *one* quality he had, but a mesh of several...the superb physical attributes of his tall, broad frame; wide-boned facial features comprising broad cheekbones, a wide, sensual mouth framed by a groove which slashed each cheek and a strong jaw. Tiny lines fanned out from the far corners of his eyes...eyes which held a dark, mesmerising intensity.

There was a degree of ruthlessness beneath his sophisticated persona, a leashed strength which boded ill for an adversary.

Yet he displayed unlimited patience with Ben, and a gentle affection which touched her deeply.

It made her wonder how he'd be with the woman to whom he'd trust his heart, his soul.

Possessive. Passionate. Primitive.

More than most women could handle.

A faint shiver shook her slender frame, and her eyes dilated as she caught the faint lift at the edge of his mouth. Almost as if he could read her thoughts…and was mildly amused by them.

Later, when Ben was asleep, she decided to lose herself in her writing again, directing fictional characters with ease through one scene and on to another…working so late, it was after midnight when she saved to disk, closed down her computer, showered and slid into bed.

It became a familiar pattern throughout the following days, with much of her writing work achieved in the evening hours as Ben slept.

The days Ben attended kindergarten Taylor collected him and went on to a park, and there were his regular swimming lessons, practice sessions she supervised in the covered swimming pool at Dante's mansion.

She followed Casey's example teaching Ben his alphabet and numbers, and they read together before dinner. After which she logged on to the

computer for the customary connection with
Dante via web-cam.

'When are you coming back?' Ben queried
during one such session a week after Dante
had flown out.

'Soon. A few days.'

'We miss you. Don't we, Taylor?'

Out of the mouths of babes! She wanted to
make the correction, assure that while Ben might,
she wasn't in the least affected by his absence.

'Of course.'

Taylor caught Dante's smile, the faint musing
gleam apparent, and knew he'd accurately
guessed her thoughts.

Later, when Taylor closed the book after she
finished reading Ben's bedtime story, she
listened to the simple prayer Casey had taught
him, then she bent low and kissed his cheek.

'Do you think Mummy and Daddy know you
and Zio are looking after me?' he queried wistfully, and she felt an arrow of pain pierce her heart.

'I'm sure they do.'

'If they're looking down from heaven, will
they see I'm in Dante's house?'

She blinked rapidly to still the warm moisture threatening to well in her eyes. 'Yes,' she managed simply and glimpsed his sweet smile as his eyelids began to droop.

'I love you, Taylor.'

It took effort to keep her voice even. 'Love you right back,' she assured gently.

She adjusted the dimmer switch to a bare glow, waited to see if he stirred, then when he didn't she quietly left the room and closed the door.

Childish simplicity cut straight to her emotional heart and wrought images of a past when life had seemed *normal*…until the night a fateful assault had put fear in her heart and had torn her emotions to shreds.

Even now, two years down the track, events of that night were startlingly vivid…and she shivered, wrapping her arms about her body in an attempt to still the images flooding back to haunt her. She could still feel the man's hard fingers pinching her flesh and the fear that had engulfed her body. She wondered now whether she would ever be able to bear the touch of any man again and her mind instantly drifted to

Dante. The few times he had touched her had sent a very different sensation through her body, and one she didn't want to analyse in too much detail.

Work was a panacea. One of the very few distractions that helped set her mind back on an even keel, and she entered her home office, opened her current manuscript file, reread a few pages to fit herself back in the scene, then she tuned out everything except the characters and the direction in which she wanted to take them.

Time had little meaning as the scene developed, engaging her total focus, and she kept up an enviable momentum as the words flowed onto the screen.

The only distraction was Ben's cough via the electronic monitor, the faint rustle of bedclothes as he turned in his sleep...followed by silence.

Taylor continued working, lost in the fictional world of her creation, aware on a subliminal level of the lateness of the hour from the weary drag of her shoulders and the dryness of her eyes.

Time to pack it in for the night...just as soon as she concluded the current chapter, she promised silently.

With effort she stretched her spine, rolled her shoulders and flexed her fingers, aware it would help if she could also flex her brain power.

Just…finish the page, then close down.

She was almost there when a faint noise broke her concentration, and she automatically glanced up, unsure if the sound emitted through the monitor—or elsewhere in the house.

Then she saw the tall male figure outlined in the doorway…and she cried out in shocked surprise, his name on her lips a barely audible gasp as he stepped into the room.

Dante took in her dilated eyes, the pale features that had, in that momentary instant, expressed real fear, and for a brief second his own eyes hardened, then became deliberately bland.

He'd managed a few hours' sleep during the flight. Enough to attune his body clock back to Australian time, enhanced by a shower and change of clothes on board.

His intention to move quietly into his own quarters had been hindered by examination of the sensor alarm…and the discovery that Taylor's office was occupied.

The possibility she might be working at this late hour seemed remote.

'I knocked,' Dante offered quietly. 'Presumably you didn't register the sound.'

She had...she just hadn't correlated it to *him*.

'What are you doing here?' Oh, hell, she sounded accusatory, almost as if she had a right to question his movements.

This was *his* home, and he didn't need to answer to her for anything.

'I—didn't think you'd be back until tomorrow,' she said in explanation, watching warily as he crossed the room and slid a hip onto the edge of her desk.

'It *is* tomorrow.'

This close he was too much, too male...and she fought against the need to push back her chair, proffer a hurried 'goodnight' and escape.

It was late, and his presence seemed to reduce the spacious room to a confined space.

Reflex action caused her to check her watch... close her eyes at the time displayed, then she opened them again, pressed the *save* key and shut the computer down.

It was late. No wonder she'd felt akin to an ant attempting to roll a stone uphill.

Taylor rose to her feet…not a good move, as it brought her too close to Dante, and she fixed her attention on a framed print on the wall to the right of his left ear.

'I should go to bed.'

His expression remained unchanged, and she took a backward step as he captured her chin between thumb and forefinger.

'Who was he?'

She felt her eyes widen at the silky query, and her stomach fluttered as if a host of butterflies beat their wings in protest. 'Excuse me?'

'The man who hurt you.'

Dear God…*no*, a silent voice screamed inside her head as dark images crowded her mind, sharpening into vivid focus.

She tried to turn her head aside, and failed miserably. 'Please—don't do this.' Her need to flee was paramount, and her eyes unwittingly beseeched he release her.

Without success, and she stood captured by the mesmerising quality apparent in his dark gaze.

Instead, he smoothed a gentle thumb over her lower lip and applied light pressure to its trembling centre. 'You have nothing to fear from me, Taylor.'

No? He had to be joking!

How could she fear this man's touch...yet inwardly crave it with an aching intensity? To fall prey to such irrational emotions was insane.

What, in the name of several patron saints, had rendered her so acutely vulnerable?

The late hour? Extreme tiredness...exhaustion?

Or was the love scene she'd just written responsible for stirring impossible yearnings?

Whatever, she dismissed wearily. The man, her reaction...it was surreal.

One thing was sure. She couldn't stay.

'Please—'

Dante lowered his head and brushed his lips to her own, sensed them part in surprise, captured her faint gasp and caught the soft fullness of her lower lip between his teeth, nipped a little, then soothed it with the edge of his tongue before lifting his head.

She looked slightly stunned and vaguely

bereft, and his eyes darkened at her visible effort to retain a sense of composure.

The temptation to pull her close and thoroughly kiss her was uppermost. There was a need to recapture the sweetness of her mouth, explore and taste with persuasive skill in an attempt to awaken her unbidden reaction.

The fact he could…easily, would be taking an unfair advantage.

Instead, he cupped her face, smoothed a light thumb over her trembling mouth, then released her.

'Go to bed,' he bade quietly. 'And get some sleep.'

Taylor was incapable of moving. Her lips parted, but no words emerged, then a strangled sound escaped from her throat, and she brushed past him.

It was only when she reached the safety of her own suite that her breathing began to slow, and she sank into a comfortable chair and buried her face in her hands.

Reaction set in, shattering the fragile tenure of her control, and the tears trickled down her cheeks until her emotions ran dry.

It was a long time before she rose wearily to her feet, discarded her clothes and stood beneath the shower in an attempt to relax the tenseness of body and mind before, dry, she pulled on cotton sleep trousers, added a sleep T-shirt and crawled beneath the bedcovers.

The next morning she could still feel the after-effects of Dante's kiss and the journey to Ben's kindergarten was made in somewhat of a daze. Determined to shake the feeling and emotions, Taylor was intent on putting in a few hours' work, and she'd barely opened the laptop when the insistent peal of her mobile phone sounded loud in the room.

She retrieved it from her bag, checked caller ID and took the call. 'Sheyna. How are you?'

'More to the point, how are *you*?' the lilting voice demanded.

Two young girls who'd met at kindergarten, clicked and formed a friendship which saw them through school, the awkward teens and into adulthood. Polar opposites...Taylor, the quiet, studious one, while Sheyna's flamboyant ex-terior hid a caring heart.

'It's been a busy week.' A slight understatement, if ever there was one.

'I get that. Meet me for coffee and fill me in.'

It was on the tip of her tongue to say she couldn't make it, only to renege. 'OK. Name the place and I'll be there in half an hour.'

Ten minutes later she'd changed into jeans, exchanged a T-shirt for a tailored shirt, pulled on boots, then twisted her hair into a knot and fastened it with a large tortoiseshell clasp and added lipstick. Then she ran lightly downstairs and out of the house to meet her oldest friend.

Sheyna had nominated a café at Darling Harbour, and they arrived almost simultaneously, hugged, chose a table and ordered coffee from a hovering waitress.

'How are you?' Sheyna began. '*Really*, without the polite platitudes.'

'OK. Getting there,' Taylor admitted. 'It'll take a while, I guess.'

Sheyna's eyes softened. 'Yes, it will. And Ben?'

'We're maintaining his usual routine, and have set up counselling. He has a puppy and a kitten.'

Sheyna lifted a hand, palm outwards. 'Back up a bit. *We?*'

'Dante, Leon's brother. We're sharing custody of Ben in a house Dante owns at Watson's Bay.'

Simple was never going to do it, and Sheyna didn't disappoint.

'I get the sharing custody bit...but sharing a house? *Dante?*' Eyebrows rose and eyes rolled in expressive appreciation. 'So what goes?'

'Nothing.'

'Darling,' Sheyna said with exaggerated patience. 'Dante d'Alessandri? *Please.*'

'It's a large house,' Taylor explained. 'He has one wing, Ben and I another. Besides, Dante travels a lot. He's away more often than he's home.'

'It had to be his idea you share the house.' Sheyna's eyes narrowed. 'Something you wouldn't have agreed to easily, but conceded to for Ben's sake. So what's Dante's motive?'

Straight to the point, no variations, just punch it out.

'Does he have to have one?' Taylor queried. 'Other than ensuring Ben settles into a stable, caring environment?'

'The man's known to be a brilliant strategist. He'll have a plan, and,' Sheyna added, 'you'll form part of it.'

The waitress delivered their coffee, and Taylor took a sugar tube, broke it and stirred in the brown crystals. 'Other than as a combination aunt-mother figure to Ben?' She shook her head. 'You're on another planet.'

Sheyna spread her hands. 'We'll see. And if I'm wrong, I'll—'

'Eat your hat?'

'Make a five-hundred-dollar donation to your charity of choice.'

'Done.' Taylor sipped her coffee, then replaced the cup. 'Your turn to play catch-up. Is Rafe still in favour?' Sheyna changed the men in her life with amazing regularity.

'Occasionally. When he conforms.'

Taylor couldn't help but smile. 'He's Spanish,' she said with a light shrug. 'You can't expect him to conform.'

'I tell him to get lost, but he keeps coming back.'

'Interesting.'

'Don't start,' Sheyna groaned. 'My mother likes him.'

'Well, then.'

'She thinks I've met my match.'

Taylor's smile widened. 'And have you?'

'He's too—' Sheyna hesitated, when she *never* hesitated '—much,' she allowed at last.

'Yet you're still seeing him?'

'Yes. Damn him.'

It was difficult to hold back a broad grin. 'I'm inclined to agree with your mother.'

'Let's finish our coffee and walk, shall we?'

They did, choosing to explore shops and displays until it was time for Taylor to leave to collect Ben.

'Keep in touch,' Sheyna bade with a friendly hug. 'Even if it's just a text message or email. OK?'

'Same goes.'

CHAPTER FIVE

IT WAS almost a week later, not long after Ben had settled to sleep for the night, that Dante chose to drop a verbal bombshell.

They were in the kitchen as Taylor poured freshly made coffee into two mugs, given they each intended to retreat in seclusion and work for a few hours.

'My mother has suggested Ben spend a vacation in Tuscany.'

Taylor's body stilled as she absorbed his words. *Tuscany*…he intended to take Ben to Italy?

Her mind spun at the mere thought of Ben being in a strange place with people he barely knew.

'It's much too soon to consider an overseas trip,' she protested. 'Ben isn't familiar with your mother. He doesn't speak the language, and he's happily settled *here*.' She tucked a stray lock of hair behind an ear. 'Wouldn't it be more sensible for her to visit Sydney?'

'My mother suffers from a fear of flying,' Dante reminded. 'She required medical sedation in order to travel to Leon's funeral. If you recall, I accompanied her on both flights.'

She'd forgotten, and had to admit it provided a different perspective. 'Doesn't your mother live in a city apartment? Ben is used to open spaces, both here—' she gestured towards the outside grounds '—and in playgrounds and parks.'

'Florence has its share of both,' he offered drily. 'It's my intention to spend most of our time at my vineyard.'

He owned a vineyard?

'Among the Tuscan hills, south of the city at Montepulciano,' Dante elaborated.

She had an instant vision of uniform rows of vines, green against the earth, tall lines of cypress trees bordering the property boundaries, gardens, and a spacious villa with a cream and terracotta-tiled roof. A dog or three, a cat or two, and room to explore. Ben would be in his element.

'Ben should have the opportunity to bond with his grandmother,' Dante pursued. 'And vice versa, don't you agree?' He didn't give her time to comment. 'He's heir to the d'Alessandri corporation, which has its origins in Italy, and it's important he be made aware of his heritage.'

Taylor viewed him with growing consternation. 'He's only *three*.'

'Almost four,' he corrected. 'At a similar age my father took me in to his office and introduced me to staff.'

She couldn't keep a degree of scepticism from her voice. 'Were you ever permitted to be a child?'

'Of course.'

'I'm relieved to hear it.'

'Unless you have a valid objection, I'd like to leave within the next few days. I assume you have a passport?'

'Excuse me?'

'Naturally you'll join us.'

'You have to be joking.'

'There's no question I'd consider travelling without you.' He began pre-empting every argument she could present, including the pressure of meeting a deadline. 'Bring your laptop and any reference material you'll need.'

She had nowhere to go...even her passport was current.

'Do you always ride roughshod over everyone?' It was difficult to minimise her acerbic tone as she glared at him.

One eyebrow lifted a little. 'Perhaps I enjoy our verbal sparring?'

Taylor raised a matching eyebrow. 'Because every other woman in your life falls over backwards to agree with you?'

'It makes for a pleasant change.'

'In that case...*hooray* for me.'

Dante speared her with a faintly mocking gaze. 'You do realise some man is going to take that fine spirit of yours and tame it.'

His words took hold of her emotions and scattered them every which way but loose. 'No chance.'

So saying, she took her coffee to her home office, and worked until late.

Dante relayed their travel plans to Ben over breakfast next morning, and Taylor could only admire his skill in the telling, for in a few simple sentences he turned the visit into an adventure. Added to which he gave a firm promise that Anna and Claude would take good care of Sooty and Rosie while they were away.

The clincher, Taylor conceded, was the prospect of flying in Dante's private luxury Gulfstream jet. The bonus being they were due to leave *soon*.

There were, however, *details*...such as the proposed length of the visit, a check of climate conditions, and whether there would be any social occasions.

Questions which Dante dismissed with a casual... 'Three, maybe four weeks. Similar temperatures. Pack light. Whatever you forget can be bought in Florence.'

She merely rolled her eyes at him. 'You might have a wardrobe in various residences around the world. I don't.'

Ben's excitement prevailed that day and the next as Taylor sorted his clothes, her own, shopped for a few essentials, then packed Ben's things in one case, and her own in another.

There was a bag with books, colouring pencils, a board game and a few DVDs to keep Ben entertained during the flight.

As it was, she needn't have bothered, for Ben was entranced from the moment they boarded. Dante introduced him to the pilot, explained a few gauges on the instrument panel before leading him into the main cabin, ready for take-off.

It was a long flight, although by observing Australian time, they were only in the air a few hours before the attendant served dinner, and it wasn't long afterwards that excitement and tiredness took their toll. The comfortable chair reclined into a bed, and Taylor carefully removed Ben's trainers, placed a pillow beneath his head, covered him with a blanket and dimmed the overhead light.

A film ran on the display screen, and she watched for a while, unaware when she fell asleep, only that when she stirred through the night she discovered her chair had been lowered and someone had added a blanket.

Dante?

The cabin lights were dimmed; a brief glance

revealed Dante intent on checking data on his laptop. Taylor merely closed her eyes and drifted back to sleep.

The switch to a different time-zone meant they touched down in Florence late afternoon, and after clearing Customs they were transported by chauffeured limousine to Dante's mother's apartment situated on the uppermost floor of a restored *palazzo* owned, Dante revealed, by the d'Alessandri corporation. The two lower levels had been tastefully renovated into self-contained units alternately rented or leased to visiting tourists.

A private lift transported them to what amounted to the penthouse, where Graziella greeted them with open affection.

An attractive woman of average height in her early seventies, immaculately attired, with kind, if faintly sad eyes.

This was no matriarch, Taylor perceived, although there was strength apparent…and genuine warmth as Graziella welcomed them in to a spacious lounge with exquisite antique furniture, beautiful paintings and cabinets showcasing delicate crystal and porcelain.

'There are refreshments, and after I will show you to your rooms. Ben, come sit close and tell me what you thought of your flight.'

Magic words, which drew descriptive detail, politely at first, then with boyish enthusiasm.

Taylor began to relax a little, allowing some of her apprehension to subside as she sampled a proffered platter comprising cheeses, crackers, bite-size portions of fresh fruit, and opted for tea instead of wine.

The apartment, on inspection, appeared to be divided into three sections, with Graziella's private rooms occupying one third. The lounge, formal dining room, informal sitting room and kitchen were centrally located, with three guest suites leading off from a passage-way to the right.

Beautifully appointed throughout, the guest suites reflected exquisite taste. Dante occupied one, and Taylor and Ben shared a suite comprising two bedrooms with a central shared *en suite*.

There was time to unpack and shower before dinner...a meal during which Graziella posed the necessity for Dante's attendance at a charity function sponsored by the d'Alessandri corporation.

'It is unfortunate timing, *caro*,' Graziella indicated with a philosophical lift of her shoulders. 'But important that you attend. I have declined out of respect to family bereavement. You will escort Taylor as your partner for the evening, and Ben shall stay with me.'

Whoa. 'I don't think—'

'Of course we'll attend.' Dante's intervention was smooth as silk.

We sounded a little too…together, and Taylor shot him a quick glance, which he appeared to ignore.

'I thought perhaps a dinner before we leave for Montepulciano,' Graziella posed. 'My brother, his wife and son. Your father's sister and her daughter. I will host it. Ben should meet his Italian family, don't you think?'

'I agree. Is it too much of an imposition to request you arrange it soon? I want to relocate to the vineyard in a matter of days.'

Dinner with family was a perfectly reasonable suggestion…but partnering Dante to a charity function undoubtedly attended by some of the city's social élite?

They needed to talk! Except the opportunity to conduct a private conversation was almost impossible. Added to which he absented himself at the d'Alessandri city office the next day, returned late after dining with business associates, and had already left for the office when Taylor and Ben joined Graziella for breakfast the following morning.

She could almost believe he was being deliberately elusive, and she was tempted to call his mobile…only to dismiss the option as the day progressed.

The evening would prove equally impossible for any private discussion, given Graziella was hosting the proposed family dinner.

Preparations involved much of the day, with the menu comprising lasagne, thin slices of veal coated with flour and dipped in beaten egg, then rolled in breadcrumbs and quickly fried. An assortment of steamed vegetables. A dessert to die for.

Graziella accepted Taylor's help, and they

chatted companionably while Ben was happily ensconced viewing a DVD.

'Family is important, don't you agree?' Graziella posed gently as she layered pasta, meat sauce and bechamel to build the lasagne.

'It's the glue which holds everything together,' Taylor responded simply.

'Especially so as both you and Casey lost your parents at a young age. You are very *simpatico* with Ben. He adores you.'

'He's a wonderful little boy.'

Graziella's hands moved with a skilled fluidity Taylor could only admire.

'For whom you have chosen to devote your life. It says much for your character. Your heart.'

What could she say, except—'Thank you'?

Graziella placed the completed lasagne dish into the oven, then together they dealt with the various pots and tidied the kitchen.

'Now we share coffee, then we bathe and change ready to receive the family.'

The formal dining-room table was set with exquisite lace over white linen, fine bone china and crystal, silver cutlery.

Redolent aromas permeated the air as Taylor checked the slim jade silk sheath she'd chosen to wear, added stilettos, swept her hair into an elegant knot secured with a fashionable clasp, decided her make-up should remain understated, and turned to regard Ben with smiling approval.

'Handsome, definitely.' Long trousers, tailored shirt, a fashionable jacket, his hair groomed to within an inch of its life, he bore the look in miniature of the man he would become. A d'Alessandri male, in the mould of his father and uncle.

There was no need to remind him of his manners...Casey had ensured he'd mastered them perfectly.

'Ready?'

'I guess.' He looked beyond her towards the door. 'Dante's here!'

Taylor turned, saw him poised in the aperture, noted his formal attire, the ready smile...and felt her heart bump a little against her ribs.

Crazy!

'My uncle and his family have arrived. Shall we go meet them?'

Pleasant, friendly people, who conversed in

English, welcomed Ben and engaged Taylor in conversation as if she were part of the family and not merely a guest.

Which was nice. A little awkward was Dante's cousin Giuseppe, who seemed intent on playing the charming admirer, which resulted in a dark, warning look from Dante, immediately followed by cousin Isabella's droll reminder.

'Taylor is with Dante. End of story.' She spared Taylor a faintly wry apologetic smile. 'Giuseppe is the biggest flirt.'

With him? Is that what they thought? Taylor opened her mouth to refute it, only to close it again in shock as Dante's hand closed over her thigh in silent warning.

'I suggest you amuse yourself elsewhere.' Dante's voice was pure silk, causing an electric silence, then Giuseppe effected a graceful shrug.

Graziella's brother complimented the lasagne, Isabella noted the wine, and the moment passed, seemingly forgotten.

Not, however, by Taylor, who smiled, conversed, pleased when Ben spoke for himself without prompting…and silently willed the evening to end.

Settling Ben into bed provided a welcome break, although not alone, as Dante joined her and read part of a bedtime story.

There was a one-minute window between closing the door to Ben's suite and rejoining Graziella and her guests…and no time at all in which to begin an argument.

To compound it, Dante linked her hand in his and did the unforgivable by raising her hand to his lips as they entered the lounge, where Graziella was in the process of serving coffee.

What was he trying to prove?

Eventually the evening came to an end, and everyone left.

'Go to bed,' he bade gently as Graziella began gathering cups and saucers together. 'Taylor and I'll tidy up and see to the dishes.'

'Please,' Taylor endorsed. 'It was a beautiful meal. You went to a lot of trouble. Thank you.'

'My pleasure.' She hesitated, then gestured to the coffee-table. 'Are you sure? I can—'

Dante leant forward and brushed his lips to Graziella's cheek. 'Sure. Goodnight.'

The various pots and pans had already been

cleaned and put away, and there was only the chinaware, crystal and cutlery that needed to be rinsed and placed in the dishwasher.

'Nothing to say?' Dante queried as they worked for several minutes in silence, and she deliberately refrained from looking at him.

'I'm waiting until only the cutlery remains. I need to resist the temptation to break a dish or three over your head.'

'You're upset.'

'You can tell?' Her voice dripped with ice, and her anger intensified when he smiled. 'I don't find it in the least amusing. They assume we're—'

'Together? We're not?'

He was teasing her, and she threw him an angry glance.

'You know precisely what I mean.'

'And it bothers you?'

'Kissing my hand…what was that?'

He caught hold of her shoulders and pulled her close. She didn't have time to blink as his mouth closed over hers, angled a little and went in deep.

One hand moved to hold fast her nape, while the other slid down to cup her bottom.

Her head spun as he savoured her, and she instinctively clutched hold of his arms in case she fell in a heap at his feet.

She lost all sense of time and place, for there was only him, the electric, all-consuming passion that tossed her high, and she groaned, heard it on some subconscious level, and tentatively met the demand of his tongue as it led an evocative dance with her own.

Nothing had come close to this. Ever.

It was almost too much.

Perhaps he sensed it, for he gentled his touch, soothing the soft inner fullness of her mouth, then brushed his lips across her own, nibbled a little, then he lifted his head, looked at her shocked expression and murmured something she didn't catch beneath his breath as he pressed her head to his chest.

'I'm sorry...I just came to check I switched off the oven.'

Taylor registered Graziella's voice as if through a distant haze, and she froze, barely aware of the hand that soothed a slow, sweeping path over the length of her spine.

She felt his lips brush the top of her head, and she pushed against him in a bid to step away from him.

'How could you?' The words emerged as a shocked whisper, and her eyes glazed as he framed her face and gently soothed a thumb over each cheek. 'Graziella will think—' She faltered, unable to finish, and saw his mouth curve into a gentle smile.

'It matters little.'

'Yes, it—'

He halted her words by the simple expediency of placing a finger to her lips. 'You're wrong.'

She wanted to cry, and almost did. 'Please…' She didn't know what she was pleading for, except the need to be alone, and he let her go, watching as she fled as swiftly as if the devil himself were at her heels.

After a few minutes he turned back to the counter, completed stacking the dishwasher, wiped down the counter-top, then he dealt with security, the lights, and moved towards his suite.

The door to Taylor's suite was closed, and he entered his own, shed his clothes, then he slid beneath the bedcovers, crossed his arms together behind his head and reflected on her response.

Unbidden, warm, passionate. More than he had expected. Enough to leave him aroused and wanting.

CHAPTER SIX

A FASHION consultation with Graziella regarding suitable attire to wear to the charity event resulted in Taylor choosing an elegant full-length fitted gown in red silk with a demure neckline and cap sleeves. It had the effect of enhancing the creamy texture of her skin, and an upswept hair-style exposed the delicate shape of her nape.

A delicate diamond pendant with matching ear-studs comprised her only jewellery, and red stilettos completed the outfit.

Graziella's approval was equally met by Dante's appreciative glance, and Ben's vocalised boyish enthusiasm.

'We should leave,' Dante indicated as he brushed his lips to Graziella's cheek, then he swept Ben high for a goodnight hug, before setting him down on his feet. 'Look after Nonna.'

'We're going to watch *Shrek* on DVD.'

Taylor leant down and kissed him. 'Love you.'

'You, too,' Ben responded at once.

The nerves which had taken root as she had dressed began to develop as she rode the lift down to the lobby, worsened slightly as the chauffeured limousine eased through the streets towards their destination.

It didn't help when Dante reached for her hand and threaded her fingers through her own, then soothed the fast-beating pulse at her wrist.

'You have no need to be nervous.'

'What makes you think I am?'

The limousine slowed and turned into the forecourt of a gracious hotel.

'Will it help if I assure you I'll remain by your side for the entire evening?'

Given *he* was responsible for almost all her nervous tension, his assurance really didn't cut it.

She was saved from responding as the limousine slid to a halt, her door opened by a uniformed concierge Dante greeted with due reverence as he moved to her side and escorted her into the lobby.

It was, Taylor observed with a degree of trepidation as they mingled with fellow guests, a very splendid event.

Sparkling jewellery adorned every designer-gowned woman present, and there was the aura of wealth…old and new.

Dante's presence garnered interest and, unless she was mistaken, a degree of speculation. There were introductions to people who expressed sympathy for their recent loss. A moment when a fellow guest captured Dante's attention, whereupon he excused himself and stepped a few paces away.

'Such a tragedy,' a matronly woman sympathised. 'To lose a son and daughter-in-law, so young. Graziella mourns their loss dreadfully. *Grazie di Dio* the little one was spared.'

What could Taylor do but offer a few suitable words in agreement?

The woman's gaze swept the groups conversing near by. 'Ah, Dante has managed to extricate himself,' she declared with an animated laugh.

Taylor turned slightly and summoned a brilliant smile.

She glimpsed the faint darkness apparent in his eyes as he read her expression, then it was gone.

'My apologies. A colleague,' he explained, turning towards the woman at Taylor's side. 'Angelina.' His greeting held friendly courtesy. 'Your presence at any event is always a bonus.'

'*Grazie*,' Angelina acknowledged. 'May I offer you both my congratulations on your forthcoming marriage?'

Marriage? What on earth was Angelina talking about?

Perhaps it was Taylor's startled expression that resulted in an explanation.

'You were unaware of the article in the media?' Angelina frowned slightly. 'You do not understand Italian? Of course!' she exclaimed. 'Allow me to explain—the article notes Dante's arrival in Florence, tonight's event, confirms the custody arrangements of Leon's son, together with the rumour of a possible marriage.'

Taylor waited for Dante to refute it, and her eyes flew wide as he took hold of her hand and lifted it to his lips. 'It is a sensible solution, *perche*?'

You have to be kidding.

He fielded her silent communication by the simple gesture of pressing a finger to her mouth. 'When it takes place it will, of course, be a very private celebration.'

'Naturally.'

He retained hold of Taylor's hand, and gave no sign when she dug her nails in *hard*.

'If you'll excuse us?'

A subtle hint...sufficient to sow the speculative seed with the media. There could only be one person...

'Graziella—'

'Has been questioned, and conceded something she said was possibly misconstrued.'

She looked at him carefully. 'You believe that?'

'I believe my mother sees a marriage between us as providing a solution.'

'A solution to *what*, precisely?'

'Formalising our present living arrangements—'

'I don't *believe* this.'

'And becoming Ben's legal adoptive parents,' he concluded, watching the green flecks in her eyes become accentuated as she attempted to control her anger.

Had this eventuated because Graziella had witnessed them kissing in the kitchen?

If so, it was unconscionable!

'You would actually *sanction* such a thing?'

'We share the same home, we're committed to raising Ben as our own.'

'Do you have any idea how hard I'm trying not to *hit* you?'

'Need I remind you we're in a public place?'

'You have, of course, insisted a retraction be printed in the media?' Taylor countered fiercely.

'Not as yet.'

'But you will.'

'Damage control?'

Her body simmered with barely controlled anger. 'Don't prevaricate.'

'Is that what you think I'm doing?'

She could leave. Turn and walk away from him, summon a taxi and return to Graziella's apartment.

A fine plan...except she didn't know the address.

Dante watched the fleeting expressions cloud

her eyes, the latent flecks burn green as she fought for control.

'Eventually the evening will end,' she managed with remarkable calm.

None too soon, she vowed as she stood at Dante's side and fielded 'good wishes' as the news spread.

For the next hour she smiled and echoed *grazie* until her jaw ached, and bore the light touch of Dante's hand at the back of her waist.

Occasionally his hand shifted lightly up her spine, rested there, only to ease across her ribs to a position just beneath the curve of her breast.

A slight upward move of his fingers and they'd touch the sensitive swell, and the breath hitched in her throat at the thought he might dare to take the liberty…accidently on purpose.

Why was it that he had only to touch her, and her entire body reacted as if to an electric charge?

Did he know?

Dear heaven, she hoped not. The mere thought caused her muscles to tense, and she felt his gaze fasten momentarily on her features…which she refused to meet.

There was relief when he moved his arm. Short-lived, as he took hold of her hand, threaded his fingers through her own, and began stroking his thumb-pad over the fast-beating pulse at her wrist.

The temptation to wrench her hand away was uppermost, and his fingers tightened, almost as if he sensed the possibility.

Dante leant his head close and murmured, 'Just a little longer, then we can escape.'

Taylor turned towards him and offered a stunning smile. 'Hallelujah.'

'Careful, *cara*. You're almost verging on overkill.'

'Really? I consider my actions quite circumspect by comparison.'

His faint, husky laugh almost undid her, and she fixed him with a vengeful glare. 'You'll keep.'

Such a sweet mouth, he mused, and so totally at variance with the words issuing from it.

He had a strong urge to watch the green flecks in her hazel eyes turn to emerald fire, and he lowered his head and sought her lips with his own, sensed her shock, savoured briefly, then went in deep.

Seconds, several of them, seemed an eternity

as she felt her body melt beneath his skilled touch. The blood sang in her veins, bringing her to vibrant, pulsing life, and she lost all sense of time and place.

Possession, she registered on some dim, distant level. Almost as if he was staking a claim.

Intense, riveting, and she instinctively reached for his shoulders and held on. The room and the people occupying it no longer existed as a deep, curling sensation settled deep in her body, radiating with an intensity that shook her slim frame and rendered her helpless.

When he lifted his head she could only look at him, her eyes dark, huge, enmeshed in an emotion so complex she dared not attempt to define it.

'That was unforgivable,' Taylor managed shakily.

'The fact I chose to kiss you?'

A kiss…that was just a *kiss*? She opened her mouth, but no sound emerged, and she closed it again, distraught to have temporarily lost the power of speech.

'Yes.'

His expression was unreadable, his eyes so dark they appeared almost black, and she was held captured, almost mesmerised by his sensual power…and its effect.

'I think we should leave.'

Ice and heat…she was fighting both, and slowly losing the battle. For two years she'd encased her emotions in ice in the need to feel *safe*. She had her family, a loving sister and nephew, and a career she loved. She told herself her life was complete.

Yet in the space of a heartbeat, all that had changed.

Now she was *here*, in Tuscany, flung together with a man who seemed intent on turning life, as she knew it, upside down.

The fact he *could* rocked her very being.

It made her want to run as far and as fast as her legs would carry her…yet, conversely, there was a part of her that whispered for her to stay. To take what he offered and enjoy the ride.

Yet caution warned of the consequences… when, not *if*, the ride ceased. As it must, eventually. What then?

And there was Ben. Her commitment to raise him to adulthood…assuming the role of the mother he'd so recently lost.

How could she face a life with Dante in it…but at odds and distant with *her*? Polite calls from his current personal assistant arranging suitable dates for transferring Ben from her care to *his*. The occasional verbal contact which would tear her apart…

'Dante, Taylor—*buona notte.*'

She heard the voices, saw friendly faces, and smiled as Dante threaded his way through the guests towards the door, conscious of the covert looks, the politely veiled interest, and guessed what they were thinking…*get a room.*

And she silently damned herself for appearing quiescent beneath his kiss…when in truth he'd taken total command of her senses.

Their car waited outside the entrance, yet Taylor couldn't recall Dante summoning the driver, and she slid into the rear seat, fastened her seat belt, then remained silent during their return to the villa.

The words she wanted to rail at him could wait until they were alone, although the temptation to let fly almost undid her.

The fact he knew didn't help.

To say she was seething by the time the car slid to a halt adjacent the front entrance to Graziella's apartment building was an understatement.

'You are,' Taylor began with quiet vehemence the moment Dante closed the front door behind them, 'the most insufferable man I've ever known.' She whirled round to face him as he set the alarm. 'How *dare* you?'

The light sconces on the walls provided the only illumination, and she watched as he slid a hand into his trouser pocket.

Damn him…how could he appear so relaxed, so…unaffected! Almost amused.

'All this fine fury because I kissed you?'

She didn't think, she simply acted, and her hand swung high in a swift arc…caught in a vice-like grip before it could connect with the left side of his face.

'Don't.'

One word, spoken with such dangerous silkiness. The sound shimmered down her body and momentarily robbed her of breath.

'I hate you.' Her voice came out as a fierce, husky sound, and angry tears glittered in her eyes.

'Almost as much as you hate yourself.'

Taylor wrenched her hand free, the words she wanted to say remaining a silent scream in her mind.

She was unprepared for the hands that cupped her face, or the soft trail of his thumb as it traversed her lower lip, and she stood helpless as he lowered his head to brush her lips lightly with his own.

A single tear escaped one eye and rolled slowly down her cheek, and she let her eyelids close in an attempt to still the shimmering moisture threatening to spill.

She felt him dispel it with his thumb, then he gently released her.

'Go to bed, Taylor,' Dante bade quietly. 'And sleep, if you can.'

He stood as she moved away, watching until she disappeared out of sight, his expression vaguely harsh in the dimmed lighting.

She stirred his blood in a manner no other woman had been able to achieve, and he ached with a desire so fierce it was only his superb control that held him back from following her.

Instead, he crossed into the kitchen, made

strong coffee and carried a cup into the library. Italy might be closed down for the night, but several international markets were not. He'd check figures and graphs on his laptop…and attempt to lose sight of the tear-stained face of the woman he wanted to take to his bed.

It crept into her mind with insidious stealth. Dark images in the depth of night, and she moved restlessly in an unconscious need to dispel the soft whispers of sound, silently begging them to cease.

Instead they persisted, teasing, taunting with what was to come.

Night, black as the devil's heart, deep as his debauched soul, ensured she saw nothing.

Only felt, instinctively, on some subconscious level, that something wasn't quite as it should be as she unlocked the front door of the house she shared with a friend.

She reached for the switch, registered the faint click, and light flooded the room.

Then she heard it, an indistinct rustling, coming from a room near by.

Go, leave, *now.*

She turned…and a hard shove sent her sprawling to the floor.

A knee jammed into the middle of her back and she cried out, using her legs in a backward kick, connecting with solid bone and muscle. Followed by a harsh male oath, then the pressure on her back ceased as the intruder rose to his feet, and hard fingers dug into her arms, flipping her onto her side.

'*Bitch.*'

A boot bit viciously into her backside, and she swiftly rolled her body in a move that took her assailant by surprise.

Except he had the advantage of standing upright, and even as she scrambled to one side she knew she couldn't escape in time to save herself.

She screamed as he dragged her to her feet, and he backhanded her with such force she almost blacked out. Then he repeated the action, and she felt the warm trickle of blood ooze from her mouth.

This wasn't happening. Not to her. She, an exponent of self-defence, knew moves that could bring a man to his knees.

Except he was too quick, too strong…and this

was *real*, not calculated practice on the tatami in a dojo. *Here* there was furniture, walls, restricted space.

She felt hands grabbing at her clothes, the tightness as he caught hold of her blouse and wrenched the front opening wide in a movement that sent buttons pinging onto the polished wood floor.

Then he reached for the snap fastening on her jeans...and she began fighting with cold, measured intent, abandoning fear for the need to survive. Creating the mindset drilled repetitively by her instructor.

It became her assailant's turn to groan with pain, to fling hoarse epithets and the threat to rape...when he got hold of her.

And he did, twisting to grasp her ankle, pulling her off-balance...and hands closed over her shoulders, a voice called her by name...

Somewhere deep in her subconscious she registered something was different, and she stilled, mentally struggling to free herself from the nightmare.

The images faded, dissipating as she reached

wakefulness…assimilating the room, the bed and the man seated on its edge.

Dante. His features vaguely harsh in the light pooling from the lamp atop the bedside pedestal. Eyes, incredibly dark, viewed her with concern…and Taylor closed her own in a gesture of defensive remorse, then slowly opened them.

'I woke you. I'm sorry.'

For a seemingly long moment he didn't say a word, merely lifted a hand to brush gentle fingers down her cheek and cup her face.

Taylor was unable to look away, and she caught her lower lip with the edge of her teeth in an unconscious gesture, oblivious to the faint stab of pain, until she felt the touch of his thumb press a soft indent, successfully causing her lips to part.

'What bothers you so badly it gives you nightmares?'

She didn't want him so close. The hastily pulled-on jeans, the black cotton T-shirt, slightly rumpled hair…the clean, fresh smell of soap mingling with the faint musk of man.

It made her long for comfort, to feel those

strong arms pull her in so her cheek rested against the beat of his heart…solid, reassuring, *caring*.

All she had to do was place her hands on his shoulders and lean in…and she almost did, except such a move would be the antithesis of common sense.

'Taylor?'

Oh, God, what could she say? And why should she even try to explain? She met his gaze, and managed to hold it. 'Please. I'm fine.'

His expression didn't change. 'You expect me to believe that?' He paused fractionally, then pursued quietly, 'You acted as if you were fighting for your life.'

Believe me, I was… Words she didn't, couldn't say.

'So,' Dante persisted gently, 'shall we start over?'

Her eyes momentarily clouded with pain. 'What if I say it's none of your business?'

'You'd be wrong.'

'Why?' Her voice sounded tortured, even to her own ears. 'You're Ben's protector. Not mine.'

'It's a package deal.'

Taylor looked at him, and glimpsed the steely

purpose beneath the silky tones. 'I'd like you to leave,' she managed with extreme care.

He dimmed the bedside lamp. 'I will, as soon as you fall asleep.'

Scandalised confusion lit her features as he moved a few feet and sank down on a nearby plush sofa. 'You can't stay there.'

'You'd prefer I share the bed?'

In one heated movement she bunched a pillow, hurled it at him with a very unladylike oath…and was thoroughly incensed by his husky chuckle as he caught the pillow and tossed it back to her.

'*You*,' Taylor said vengefully, 'are the most *impossible* man I've ever met. *Go!* Please.'

It was the *please* that got to him, together with the suddenly stark look that rendered her hazel eyes green.

He had a need to gather her in against him, assure her with touch and words that he'd permit no one to hurt her again.

Instead, he rose to his feet, inclined his head, crossed the room and closed the door quietly behind him.

She expected to remain awake, her mind filled

in equal parts with the lingering wisps of a night-mare…and Dante's unexpected presence.

Unwanted, she assured as she punched her pillow, then tossed it over and rendered another punch before resting her head down.

Except his image taunted her. His closeness, the clean male smell…her unqualified urge to nestle in against him and accept his touch.

Crazy. A brief moment of insanity on her part.

So *sleep*, why don't you? a tiny imp prompted.

And she did, slipping dreamlessly into somnolence from which she woke feeling surprisingly refreshed.

CHAPTER SEVEN

'TAYLOR. Wake up.'

The childish voice penetrated her subconscious, and she rolled over in bed, opened her eyes and saw Ben standing close to the bed.

'I'm still sleeping.'

A childish giggle was followed by a wide smile. 'No, you're not. Your eyes are open.'

She attempted a mock-stern expression. 'And what, young man, are you doing waking me up at the crack of dawn?'

Dark eyes gleamed with mischief. 'It's eight o'clock, and Dante and Nonna are having breakfast.'

Oh, my…that late. Hardly surprising when it had been late before she had slept last night. Correction, the early hours of this morning.

'Your photo is in the paper.'

That brought her into a sitting position. 'It is?'

'Dante, too. Nonna showed me.'

Last night's event had involved some of the city's glitterati. The name d'Alessandri was revered, and Dante's presence at any major social event more or less guaranteed his appearance on the social pages.

'You were kissing Dante.'

Except Ben was wrong...it had been Dante who had initiated the kiss. *She* who'd lost herself in his touch. Even now her stomach fluttered at the memory and sensation arrowed deep inside.

'Dante said we're going to his vineyard today.' Ben's eyes gleamed with anticipation. 'There's cats and dogs, and lots of grapes,' he relayed with importance.

'If you wait a few minutes, I'll get dressed, then we'll go join the others.'

'OK.'

The simplicity of childhood, Taylor mused as she moved into the *en suite*.

If she was honest, she had to admit this visit to Florence was proving successful for Ben. A change in territory, new places to explore, and most importantly an opportunity for him to bond with Dante and Graziella. To learn he was part of another culture, and accept that, although his life had undergone a change…everything would be all right.

Except…last night. The media, the socialite Angelina *whoever* offering congratulations… and, not the least of which, Dante's kiss.

Although *kiss* didn't come close to covering the frankly sensual, flagrant assault on her senses.

Even now her mouth tingled with the remembered passion of his touch.

One thing was uppermost…they needed to *talk*, and *soon*. Any nonsense about marriage had to cease and a retraction printed in the media.

She could accept combined custody, even sharing the same residence long-term. But *marriage*?

Was that what had precipitated the nightmare?

And suddenly it was *there*…all of it, resurfacing to race through her mind in kaleidoscopic detail.

Oh, dear heaven, she whispered inwardly as she caught her mirrored image. The eyes so dark, appearing large, their expression stark in a face pale as the colour leached from her cheeks.

Pull yourself together, a silent voice bade. Face the fear, and conquer it.

Easily said…not so easy to do. Except she had the benefit of practice. Relax, concentrate, focus.

Learned psychological techniques which helped her retain a sense of time and place, ensuring she completed her early-morning routine before tugging on jeans, a top, then she slid her feet into soft flat shoes and re-entered the bedroom to find Ben patiently waiting.

Dante rose to his feet as they entered the dining room, a lazy smile widening his mouth.

Taylor met his dark gaze, caught the way it lingered a little long on her mouth, and endeavoured to still the faint colour warming her cheeks. She matched Graziella's smile and offered, 'Good morning.'

Graziella reached for the coffee-pot and poured aromatic dark liquid into a cup. 'Come sit down, my dear.'

She indicated dishes under cover laid out on the chiffonier. 'Do help yourself when you're ready.'

Dante's presence had an electrifying effect, accelerating her pulse-beat and creating a heightened state of sensuality.

Dammit, she could almost *feel* the pressure of his mouth on her own, the dangerous, elemental power of his touch…and her reaction. There was a tendency to run the tip of her tongue along her lower lip in a bid to still the faint quiver hovering there.

Except to do so would merely prove she was far from immune…and she was damned if she'd give him the satisfaction.

Taylor settled for coffee and a croissant. Anything more would play havoc with her digestion.

'I thought we'd take a break from the city for a while,' Dante indicated with an easy smile, 'and spend time at the Montepulciano vineyard.'

'Pleasant countryside just under two hundred kilometres to the south east,' Graziella added. 'The vineyard produces *Vino Nobile*, considered to be among Italy's best.' She spared her son a slight smile. 'It is Dante's—' a faint frown creased her forehead '—how do you say? Escape.'

Dante as a vintner? Picking grapes in the field? *Earthy?* Somehow it didn't gel with his sophisticated image.

Taylor carefully replaced her cup down onto its saucer and offered him a studied look. 'You're proposing we stay there…for how long?'

'A week, possibly longer.' A faint gleam lightened his dark eyes. 'There are staff, and Graziella is an adequate chaperone.' He didn't add *if that's what bothers you.*

Except the implication was there, and her chin lifted a little. 'I'm sure Ben will love it.'

'Dante says I can have a bike to ride, just like the one at home, and he's going to teach me things,' Ben assured with such earnestness, it was impossible not to smile. 'And there's some dogs, and two cats.' He paused, and rushed on with excited importance. 'And maybe some new kittens.'

Taylor's expression softened, and she teased gently, 'So I guess we get to pack, huh?'

'Yes, please. Can we do it now?'

'If Taylor has finished breakfast,' Graziella chided quietly, and caught Taylor's nod in acquiescence.

'What time do you want to leave?'

'Around ten.'

Taylor checked her watch. That gave them just over an hour. 'If you'll excuse me?'

She rose to her feet, caught Ben's hand and moved from the dining room. Almost as soon as they were out of sight, Ben loosened his hold and quickened his step towards their suite of rooms.

Taylor attended to Ben's clothes first, then her own, and it was one very excited little boy who happily allowed himself to be secured in a booster seat alongside Taylor in the rear of a luxury four-wheel-drive.

Soon the city gave way to tracts of land, villages large and small, the countryside lush green, boundaries lined with cypress tees standing like tall dark green sentinels against fallow and planted fields.

There was a freshness in the air, the clean smell of the land and all it nurtured.

'Are we nearly there?'

'Soon.' Dante's voice was a mildly amused drawl, and his gaze connected briefly with Taylor via the rear-vision mirror.

Acreage of indeterminate size hugged the hills, with villas of various ages and designs. Cream and terracotta tiled roofs, cream stucco walls nestled among trees and shrubbery, gardens large and small, some with symmetry, flora in large clay pots and urns. Olive groves, vineyards, separated by meandering clay tracks.

It was into one of these tracks Dante eased the four-wheel-drive, travelling at a moderate speed between high clipped hedges and burgeoning shrubbery, then he turned a relatively tight corner...and there the villa stood, a blend of old and new, as additions had been added to the main structure over time.

Yet the whole held a captivating charm, with its wide portico, French-style doors, stone-paved walkways. Green creeper held purchase over one external wall, and the view over the gently sloping land brought a catch to Taylor's throat.

Beautiful was the first and only word that came immediately to mind. Others would follow, but beautiful was the one that would always remain in her mind.

There were sounds she barely registered...a

dog, or was it two, barking in unison as Dante brought the vehicle to a halt adjacent the front portico? And she turned at the sound of a door opening, saw a middle-aged woman framed in the doorway, smiling in welcome as Dante emerged from behind the wheel.

Greetings were exchanged, introductions complete, whereupon Dante summoned the two dogs forward…a German shepherd and a golden Labrador, and formerly instructed each dog that Taylor and Ben were friends.

A process which fascinated Ben, who obediently stood still, then tentatively extended his hand, only to laugh as first one dog, then the other, licked his fingers.

After which Dante ordered the dogs to *stay,* and led his guests indoors to a spacious entry lobby whose walls held oil paintings, wall tapestries, and solid furniture rested on a huge, multi-patterned carpet square that covered most of the tiled floor.

Hallways led off to the left and right, and a sweeping staircase led to an upper level.

'Lunch will be served in an hour,' Lena, the

housekeeper, informed in heavily accented English. 'The rooms are ready, and Mario will transfer the luggage.'

'My usual suite, Lena?' Graziella asked, and the housekeeper confirmed, adding, 'I'll take the guests to their rooms.'

The interior appeared to flow easily from one area to another, and it was Lena who led Taylor and Ben upstairs to a wing containing guest suites, each with an adjoining modern *en suite*.

'I hope you will be comfortable here.'

What isn't to like? Taylor decided with approval, and offered a warm smile. 'Thank you. You're very kind.'

'It is Signor Dante's instructions.' Lena inclined her head. 'I will leave you to freshen up.'

'Can I have the room with *two* beds?' Ben asked as soon as Lena disappeared from the room, and Taylor leant out a hand and ruffled his hair.

'I don't see why not.'

Minutes later there was a tap at Taylor's open door, and a man who introduced himself as Mario deposited two bags at the foot of her bed, then he inclined his head and retreated down the stairs.

'OK, champ, let's unpack, shall we?'

'Then can we go see the dogs?'

She checked her watch. 'Maybe after lunch. First, we need to unpack and freshen up.'

'There's a cat and kittens, too. Nonna said.'

'Lots of things for you to see and do,' Taylor teased. 'But not all in one day, huh?'

'Dante is going to take me to see the grapes, and where they make the wine, and the—'

'Cellars?'

'Yes.' His eyes grew round. 'That's where the wine is stored. In barrels.'

'You're learning fast.'

She couldn't recall precisely *when Zio* had morphed into *Dante*. A while. Natural, perhaps, when Ben had called her *Taylor* from the moment he could talk.

Lunch was a pleasant meal eaten in a conservatory-type informal dining room which offered stunning views out over the vineyard to the distant valley.

The land, spacious with its patchwork of varied colours, predominantly shades of green against the terracotta clay of the earth, and faint tinges of gold and brown leaves in deference to the approaching northern-hemispheric autumn.

It was magnificent, Taylor accorded silently. Peaceful, after the city with its bustling cosmopolitan atmosphere, people, traffic.

'August is a lovely time of year,' Graziella revealed gently. 'There is warmth in the sun, the sky a beautiful blue, and excitement in the air as the harvest of the grapes draws near.'

'Can we look for the cat and the kittens after lunch?' Ben asked eagerly, and Dante reached out and ruffled the boy's hair.

'After lunch, we observe the siesta. Just a short rest, hmm…then I'll take you and Taylor on a conducted tour.'

'Do we have to rest?'

'A quiet time, in preparation for what remains of the day,' Graziella explained. 'Otherwise you will not be able to stay awake for dinner.'

It had been relatively easy to observe that quiet time while staying in Graziella's Florence apartment. But here, where there was so much to see and do, it was difficult to get Ben to settle.

With some encouragement Taylor managed to

get him to lie down on the bed he'd selected as his own, while she read him a story.

It was almost mid-afternoon when Lena appeared and announced Dante was waiting for them downstairs.

Sunhat, shoes and sunscreen, and they were good to go, and it was Ben who needed to be held back, to walk not run as they descended the stairs to the spacious entry lobby.

Taylor's initial thought that Dante's vineyard was merely a hobby farm was quickly discounted beneath his guidance as they began with the cellars, introductions to staff, an explanation of the process from grape-picking to wine, before emerging into the sunshine and an inspection of the first row of vines, where succulent bunches of grapes ripened and matured beneath their protective leaf coverage.

Dante kept it simple and, although Taylor absorbed the words, much of her attention was taken by his close proximity and its effect on her.

The sophisticated corporate CEO was on a sabbatical, and in his place was a man dedicated to the land, *his* land. A place that owed little to billion-dollar deals on an international scale.

He even *looked* different…if that was possible.

With the absence of the formal city attire of tailored suit, buttoned shirt and tie, he bore an earthy persona in well-worn jeans, a black T-shirt moulding his impressive frame, and work boots.

Ever-present was the latent sensuality he projected with effortless ease, the intrinsic knowledge of women, how to pleasure them and the promise of being a compelling, even primitive, lover.

It was there in the lazy gleam in those dark eyes, the glimmer of shimmering heat… magnetic, evocative, *lethal.*

On one level it almost frightened her. On another it excited and made her yearn for the unobtainable.

Was he aware of her inner struggle?

She fervently hoped not.

Yet with every passing day it became more difficult to portray a friendly but distant persona.

Sharing custody of Ben was totally different from what she'd originally envisaged. Dante's degree of involvement was so much more than she had expected, or that he'd led her to believe.

In Sydney, even when he travelled on business, his presence was *there* via web-cam and phone calls.

In Italy, it was a constant. Worse, knowing Graziella was in favour of fostering their relationship.

As if that was going to happen.

Three months ago she'd been in control of her life. Yet in a short space of time she'd given up her apartment, moved into a mansion, and now here she was in Italy...all for the love of her orphaned nephew and her commitment to raise him.

None of which she regretted.

Dante d'Alessandri's involvement was something else entirely. Because *he* affected *her*...too much.

It was unsettling. And ever-present was an instinctive feeling Dante had a definite agenda.

'You're thinking too much.'

The sound of his musing drawl brought her back to the present, and she offered a wry smile.

'Just absorbing all the interesting information.'

Dante shot her a quizzical look. 'One imagines it's conclusive?'

The subtext was apparent, and she countered, 'Supposition or fact?'

His mouth curved and showed even white teeth. 'We should talk.'

Taylor looked at him carefully. 'There's nothing to say.'

'I disagree.'

A change of subject was essential, and she cast her eyes out over the many uniform rows of vines. 'It's a beautiful property.'

'Thank you.'

'Have you owned it long?'

'Nine years,' Dante revealed easily. 'The villa and buildings have been modernised, staff added to ensure the vineyard runs at a premium.'

'There's a cat!' Ben announced with excitement, and Dante smiled, directing the child's attention to a nearby outbuilding. 'If you follow her carefully, you'll be able to watch her feeding her kittens. Quietly,' he cautioned, 'so you don't disturb or frighten her.'

'Oh, boy. I'll be very careful.'

Taylor watched as he trod almost on tiptoe until both the cat and Ben disappeared, then she turned towards the man standing within touching distance.

'You love it here.' A statement, not a query.

'It's where I come to relax.'

'Do you?' she asked with a degree of cynicism. 'Relax? Ever?'

'The company of a good woman, family, provides a persuasive element.'

The mere thought conjured up an image she didn't want to contemplate. 'Marriage? All you'll need to do is crook a finger to whoever takes your fancy from a long line of willing women.'

'Indeed?'

He watched the fleeting emotions chase across her expressive features for the few seconds it took for her to control them.

There was no artifice or pretence apparent, coupled with a strength of mind he could only admire. It was her determination to fight to the bitter end for what was right for Ben…something he counted on.

She intrigued him…cool, laid-back on the surface, and in control. Except she became a chameleon in his arms, sensually *alive* in a way that made him want more, so much more than she wanted to give.

Prepared to give, he amended...and recognized the difference.

She told herself it was the warmth of the sun that caused her head to spin, and knew she lied.

It wasn't inconceivable Dante might want to marry, have his own family.

Except where would that leave Ben? *Her?*

Shared custody would take on a whole different meaning.

Moving back into her apartment wouldn't pose a problem, but what about Ben? How would he cope being shuffled between two households? And what if Dante shifted base from Sydney?

They'd be back to square one, in an identical situation when the issue of Ben's custody had first arisen.

'I trust you'll give me sufficient notice, so that Ben can be told.' She knew her voice was stiff and overly polite, but she didn't care.

He wanted to *shake* her, and barely refrained from taking hold of her shoulders and doing so. The only thing that stopped him was the possibility

Ben might witness the action. Instead his voice assumed the quality of silk-encased steel, a tone which on occasions made lesser minions tremble.

'Make no mistake,' Dante began with dangerous quietness, 'it's *you* I want as my wife.'

Taylor lifted her head slightly and met his gaze with unflinching regard. 'You're suggesting a convenient merger,' she corrected. 'Formalised by a legal certificate. And the answer is no.' She waited a beat. 'Thank you.'

Whatever reaction she expected, it wasn't a husky laugh or the humorous gleam apparent in his dark eyes.

'It's neither the time or place. But understand this,' he said quietly. 'I'm far from done.'

He lifted a hand and brushed the back of his hand down her cheek. 'Perhaps it might be a good idea to check on Ben and the kittens,' Dante suggested, turning towards the outbuilding, giving her no choice but to follow as he threaded his fingers through her own…firming his clasp as she attempted to pull free.

Although her expression softened as she entered the outbuilding and saw Ben crouched down, looking engrossed and breathing softly, beside the box where the mother cat tended her kittens.

He looked up as he sensed her presence, put a finger to his lips, then returned his attention to the box.

'There are five of them,' Dante enlightened quietly. 'Born the day before yesterday.'

Taylor moved close and rested a hand on Ben's shoulder. Five tiny heads suckled fiercely, using their front paws to knead their mother's belly.

'They're feeding,' Ben relayed importantly.

'They're beautiful,' she said quietly. Or at least they would be when they grew a little and their fur fluffed out.

'We'll keep one, and find homes for the others.'

'I'm glad.' So she had a soft heart, for animals as well as children.

'Can we stay and watch them?'

Taylor examined Ben's rapt features and inclined her head. 'Just for another minute or two. Their mother will want them to sleep soon.'

'We can check again later.' Dante leant down and lifted Ben high onto his shoulders. 'But now we're going to take a tour of the house.'

Modern blended with the old…skilfully so, owing much to the tradesmen's skill to ensure little compromised the architecture or history, Taylor perceived as they moved from room to room.

High vaulted ceilings, plastered interior walls, large terracotta-tiled floors covered in huge patterned rugs.

Formal lounge, media room, library, formal dining room, a spacious home office, a guest suite which Graziella used whenever she visited, as well as a magnificent kitchen, the conservatory-style informal dining room, and to one side of a renovated addition was a large tinted-glass-enclosed swimming pool. Upstairs comprised two distinct wings, one which Dante claimed for his own use, comprising a master suite, private lounge and a personal home office fitted with what appeared to be an array of advanced electronic technology.

The opposite wing held three guest suites, two of which Taylor and Ben occupied.

No money had been spared in the renovation upgrading, and the result was breathtaking.

'If you'll excuse me, I need to consult with the

head vintner.' He released Ben down onto his feet. 'If you ask Taylor nicely, she might allow you to ride the new bike Mario has brought around to the front entrance.'

Ben gazed up at Dante in open adoration. 'A bike? You bought me a bike?' He transferred his attention to Taylor.

'Can I ride it? *Please?*'

How could she refuse?

They spent a fun hour as Ben put the bike through its paces, followed by another peek at the mother cat with her kittens.

Dinner proved a convivial meal, with a divine pasta dish and salad served by Lena, where much of the conversation involved Ben, the vineyard, the bike, and perhaps high on his list…the cat and her kittens.

The result was one tired little boy at day's end, who fell asleep before the first page was turned of his bedtime story.

'He's having the time of his life,' Taylor offered as Dante closed Ben's bedroom door. 'Thank you.'

He was standing close, and she resisted the

temptation to step back a pace as he regarded her solemnly. 'And you, Taylor? Are you equally content here?'

What could she say? 'You have a lovely home, and the vineyard is magnificent.'

His mouth curved with humour. 'Very politely spoken.'

'You've been very generous.'

The corners of his mouth quirked a little and his eyes acquired a musing gleam. 'Better.' He lifted a hand and brushed gentle fingers down her cheek. 'Have dinner with me tomorrow night. There's a charming *trattoria* in town which serves wonderful food. You'll enjoy it.'

Her pulse kicked in to a faster beat, in betrayal, and she stood perfectly still. 'I should write. I have a—'

'Deadline,' he completed the sentence. 'You can work tomorrow. Ben will spend the morning with me.'

'It's important.' And silently damned herself for the need to justify the need.

'Your career? Did I infer it wasn't?'

She was conscious of a slight shift, an acceleration of the electric tension between them, and she took a step away from him.

'If you don't mind, I should check my emails and put in a few hours of work now.'

'By all means. There's an internet connection in the library you can use. Collect your laptop and I'll ensure you're set up correctly.'

It didn't take long, and there was a sense of awe at the size of the spacious room with its walls lined with floor-to-ceiling bookcases, two comfortable leather recliner chairs and an impressive antique desk.

'Thank you.' She spread her hands as she indicated the room. 'This is amazing.'

'Close everything when you're done. The hallways throughout the villa are on a timer and dim down to half-power at midnight.' He cupped her face, leant in and took her mouth with his own in a kiss that seared her soul.

Then he released her, his mouth curving a little at her stunned expression. 'Sleep well.'

Then he turned and walked from the room, closing the door quietly behind him.

CHAPTER EIGHT

THE following evening Dante eased the luxury four-wheel-drive towards the end of the lane linking it to the arterial road which led into the town.

'Graziella is capable of settling Ben to bed.'

Taylor glanced away from the passing scenery, the patchwork of the various fields with their rows of vineyards and the cypress bordering the road. The sky was opalescent with changing colour as the sun sank low towards the horizon. Evenings remained light much longer here during summer than they did in the southern hemisphere, and she enjoyed the slow fading of the night sky.

'I don't doubt it.'

'Yet you're unable to relax.'

Because *you* disturb me. Aloud, she admitted, 'You're not an easy person to be around.'

'And that bothers you?'

It bothered her like hell. 'I have no intention of stroking your ego.'

'Your honesty is admirable.'

He was teasing her, and if she felt more at ease with him she'd have offered a laughing response. Instead, she offered wryly, 'Count on it.'

He spared her a musing glance. 'The *trattoria* is owned by friends of mine, and situated in a small village not far from here.'

Dante parked on the village outskirts, locked the vehicle, then he caught hold of her hand and loosely threaded his fingers through her own.

She was tempted to pull free, and his clasp tightened fractionally, almost as if he guessed her intention.

It was like going back in time, Taylor mused as they trod the uneven paving, the buildings old and mellowed gold in the evening light.

There were a few people gathered at outdoor tables, talking in voluble Italian. Men, young and old, drinking espresso coffee, dark red wine, some smoking. Not many women, and those few present looked like tourists or visitors absorbing the ambience.

The air was redolent with spices, food and a hint of garlic in the cooking.

As they walked, a male voice called out a greeting, and Dante answered in his own language, pausing to exchange a few words and effect an introduction.

Taylor was aware of the thinly disguised speculation apparent, the momentary gleam of appreciation in the man's eyes…and wondered at the sophistication beneath the urbane veneer.

'A business associate?' she enquired as they continued walking, and received Dante's acknowledgment in response.

'And childhood friend. Carlo owns a vineyard a few kilometres from mine.'

Dante led her towards a charming restaurant and bar, with outdoor tables for those who preferred to eat and drink in the open.

'The food is exquisite,' he informed as they moved inside. 'Mariangela is noted for her *gnocchi*. You must try a sample.'

'*Dio madonna*,' a male voice boomed.

'Mariangela, come quickly.' What followed was lost in the flood of voluble Italian as a barrel of a man rushed forward to clasp Dante in a bear-like hug. Then a woman appeared from the kitchen, took one look at Dante, cried out and all but ran to greet him.

Dante laughed, lifted her high and swung her full circle before setting her down and effecting an introduction.

'So, you bring your woman to see us, eh?' Mariangela teased. 'What takes you so long?' She leant forward, caught hold of Taylor's shoulders and brushed first one cheek, then the other, European-style. 'Taylor. It's a beautiful name.' She stood back a pace and gestured towards a table. 'Come, sit down. Bruno will fetch the *vino*, and bring some *bruschetta*. When you ready, you order. After we talk, *sì*?'

What followed became a tableau of northern-Italian village life, Taylor perceived as she became caught up in the rich ambience...the voices, loud at times and punctuated with laughter; the aroma of fine, home-style cooked food with its many spices; the wine.

And the *food…gnocchi*, such as Taylor had never tasted before, even in the finest restaurant in Sydney. A delicate veal *parmigiana* so tender it could be cut with a fork, accompanied by a salad with exquisite dressing, followed by a superb lemon sorbet.

'I don't think I shall ever eat again,' Taylor revealed as she declined coffee in favour of tea. 'It's wonderful here. Thank you,' she added in genuine appreciation and felt her pulse quicken in reaction to Dante's warm smile.

'My pleasure. However, the evening isn't over yet.'

'You mean, there's more?'

'Bruno and Mariangela's two sons will emerge from the kitchen with their guitars and sing.'

'Really?'

Almost on cue, male voices could be heard in harmony from the kitchen, then two fine-looking young men in their late twenties emerged to a burst of applause.

Traditional songs, one after the other, interspersed with some teasing comedic humour, which brought laughter, and they were good…very good.

Taylor found herself alternately smiling and laughing, and almost wishing she were sufficiently conversant with the Italian language to sing along with the patrons.

'You won't mind if I join you?'

She turned slightly to see Carlo had approached their table, and Dante gestured he pull up a spare chair.

'Let me order another bottle of wine.'

'I think not, my friend,' Dante declined. 'I must drive, and so, too, must you.'

'A *fernet branca*, perhaps?'

'Coffee,' Dante insisted quietly.

Carlo leant back in his chair and regarded Taylor carefully. 'So, this woman must be special. It is the first one you bring to sample Mariangela's food.'

'We share custody of Leon's son.'

Bruno delivered coffee, and three snifters of spirits, enquired if everything was to their satisfaction, then retreated with a smile at their fulsome praise.

Carlo tipped a snifter of spirits into his espresso coffee. 'A sad loss.'

'Indeed.'

'And, Taylor,' Carlo offered in a teasing drawl as he indicated Dante. 'You like this man?'

'Occasionally.'

Soft laughter accompanied his gleaming gaze. 'Honesty. How refreshingly different.'

'Different from?' Taylor posed, and Carlo's eyes gleamed with humour.

'The women who usually grace Dante's arm.'

Wry humour lifted the corners of her mouth. 'There are, of course, so many.'

'Sycophants, all of them.' It was a cynical concurrence, but accompanied with underlying humour.

'Spoken from experience, I gather?'

His laughter sounded genuine. 'We should become better acquainted. Have dinner with me tomorrow evening.'

'Carlo.' One word spoken in sibilant caution by Dante was sufficient to bring speculative recognition in response. 'Taylor is with me.' The words were quietly issued, but held unmistakable ownership.

Taylor shot Dante a look which promised retribution, given the first possible moment, only to meet his deliberately bland features. Although his eyes were dark, unrepentant...fathomless.

He resonated power in its utmost form. Highly potent, relentless. A man slow to anger...but lethal in its execution.

Yet she held his gaze, refusing to be intimidated, and the air between them sizzled with electric tension, diminishing everything around them into a state of non-existence.

'So,' Carlo intoned quietly. 'The marriage rumour is true.'

Dante's eyes remained locked with her own. 'It is a consideration.' He waited a beat. 'But not yet official, *comprendere*?'

Taylor felt incapable of movement, unaware of the deep thudding of her pulse at the base of her throat or the dark green flecks surging to prominence in her eyes.

Dante evidenced both, and lifted his hand for the bill, settled it, then stood. 'If you'll excuse us?'

'Of course.' Carlo's response was cool, courteous as he rose from the table. 'It's becoming late.'

It was impossible to leave easily, for both

Bruno and Mariangela descended, whereupon a flood of voluble Italian ensued, followed by the customary 'goodnight'.

'How *dare* you?' Taylor demanded in a low voice as they trod the paved path towards Dante's four-wheel-drive.

'To what, precisely, do you refer?'

She paused and turned to face him. 'Acting like a proprietorial ass.'

She could tell little from his expression in the darkness. 'I don't recall ever being referred to in quite that manner…'

'There's always a first time!'

'*Cara*—'

'I'm not your *dear* anything.'

'Do you particularly want to fight?'

She lifted her head, anger emanating from her body in waves. 'From the beginning, you've set the pace, enforcing what happens, when and where.' Her eyes blazed searing heat. She was so wound up, it was affecting her breathing. 'Worse, you're stalling on issuing a retraction to that *ridiculous* media inference to marriage.'

'To which you object.'

Taylor looked at him in stark disbelief. 'How can you even contemplate such a thing?'

'Easily.'

Her lips parted to rail at him, and didn't succeed in uttering a further word, for the simple reason Dante slid one hand to anchor her nape and used an arm to pull her in as his mouth covered hers in a deep, almost dark kiss that took her anger and tamed it into willing submission.

There was nothing else but *him*, and his power to make her feel as if the earth had suddenly tilted on its axis, and she simply wound her arms around his neck…and held on. *Lost* in passion so intense it was almost a conflagration.

His hand slid down her back, cupped her bottom and held her fast against the hard length of his arousal.

The hand that captured her nape slid to her ribcage, then moved to her breast, shaping the rounded contour with the palm of his hand…and she wasn't aware of the faint, guttural sound that became trapped in her throat, or the way she met the thrust of his tongue, the faint edge of his teeth against the swollen softness of her lower lip.

Slowly he eased the pressure, soothing with tactile gentleness as his hands skimmed her back, caging her so she rested boneless against the strength of his body.

For what seemed an age she attempted to gather together her shattered emotions, her hands unsteady as she withdrew them slowly from his neck, and she was conscious of her breath hitching irregularly as she sought to pull away from him.

His hold was light as he rested his forehead against her own, and his breath was warm against her face.

'Are you so sure marriage between us won't work?' Dante queried quietly.

Sure? She was no longer sure of anything! Least of which the man who had all but branded her his own.

'It's an insane suggestion,' Taylor managed shakily. She lifted a hand and ran trembling fingers through the length of her hair.

He reached for her hand, felt the thudding pulse at her wrist and soothed the rapid beat with his thumb. 'You doubt I'd be an attentive husband?'

Oh, God. The mere thought of him as a lover sent her imagination soaring off the Richter scale!

For heaven's sake, *get a grip*.

'Why pursue the hypothetical?' she managed heatedly. 'There isn't going to be a marriage!'

'Not even for Ben's sake?'

Taylor closed her eyes, then slowly opened them again. 'That's coercion.'

'I prefer...persuasion.'

'Why?'

'I want a woman to bear my name, have children with me, share a lifetime.'

The thought tore her apart.

Marriage would formalise their commitment to Ben...but how was it possible to contemplate marriage without love, Taylor agonised silently, wanting the impossible, but too afraid to reach for it?

'And it may as well be me?'

'Why not you?'

'Because I won't be part of a convenient solution!'

The stars were out in an indigo sky, and there was sufficient illumination to witness his hard-boned facial features, if not to determine his precise expression.

'I don't believe convenient or solution were mentioned.'

It was too much. *He* was too much.

'I'd like to go home,' she managed evenly… difficult, when she felt as if her life was spinning out of control.

Except *home* wasn't an option. She didn't even *have* a home, she reflected wretchedly…aware her apartment didn't really count any more.

A muted beep sounded as Dante used the remote control to unlock the four-wheel-drive, and she reached for the door clasp an instant before he did, then she pulled open the door and slid into the front seat.

Seconds later he moved behind the wheel, ignited the engine, turned the vehicle and sent it in the direction of the villa.

He didn't attempt to offer anything by way of conversation, and neither did she during the drive.

Consequently it was a relief when they arrived at the vineyard and Dante garaged the four-wheel-drive.

'Thank you for a pleasant evening,' Taylor said in a stiff voice as she moved towards the internal door leading indirectly to the main living quarters.

He fell into step at her side. 'So polite,' he taunted quietly, resting a hand at the back of her waist and keeping it there until they reached the main lobby.

She would have ascended the staircase without a further word, except firm hands took hold of her shoulders and turned her towards him.

For a moment she resembled a startled doe, all eyes and on the defensive.

Dante lowered his head, touched his lips to the tip of her nose and sought the edge of her mouth in a fleeting kiss before releasing her.

Taylor stood still, unable to move for a few long seconds, then she turned and almost ran up the stairs without a backward glance.

It was a relief to enter her suite, and she carefully closed the door, conscious of her rapid breathing…something she consciously stilled before discarding her clothes and pulling on nightwear. Seconds later she crossed into the *en suite*, removed her make-up and completed her nightly routine before slipping into Ben's room to check on him.

The small figure didn't stir, and she stood looking at his features, peaceful in sleep, before retreating to her room, aware any form of *rest* would be impossible, given her conflicting state of mind.

If only…

Taylor closed her eyes, then slowly opened them again.

There was no point in listing the *if onlys*, for it served no purpose.

The only constant was the situation in which she found herself…the reality of being charged with Ben's care and sharing that care with a very disturbing man who wanted more than she was prepared to give.

Worse, he had an agenda…a very clear-cut strategy that neatly tied up several loose ends, providing stability and permanence, legally and emotionally, for the future heir of the d'Alessandri corporation.

Worse, Dante seemed bent on proving a legal union between them wouldn't prove a hardship, both in and out of the marriage bed.

An opportunity most women would jubilantly seize with both hands...for what Dante's wealth would provide, the residences in various countries, gifts, social status. Plus the bonus of a skilled and generous lover in their bed.

Many women married for less.

So why not *her*?

Marriage as commitment. *But not necessarily coupled with love*, Taylor agonised silently.

Except not everyone got everything they wanted in life.

What Dante offered...was it *enough* to sacrifice her independence?

To take a chance and be content as Dante's wife? Cement Ben's future, and add a child or two of their own?

At the end of the day it all came down to *trust*.

'*Buon giorno*, Taylor. Ben, how are you?' Lena greeted as they entered the kitchen together. 'It is a beautiful morning, and your *Nonna* is having coffee on the terrace. You go there, too, and I will bring breakfast soon.'

There was warmth in the sun, with the promise

of heat as the morning grew, and the aroma of freshly brewed coffee was enticing.

Graziella held out her arms as she sighted them, and Taylor smiled as Ben almost ran to be enfolded close, then Graziella lifted her head and gestured towards a nearby chair.

'Come. Sit with me. It is a beautiful view, is it not?'

'Stunning,' Taylor agreed as she took a seat. And it was all of that, with a clear blue sky as far as the eye could see, gently rolling land, green fields, shrubbery, the uniformity of row upon row of vines, and in the distance the tall, slender stands of cypress.

There was a sense of peace, of timelessness.

'Dante will eat with the men this morning,' Graziella revealed, casting Ben a benevolent look. 'Then he plans to take you with him for a few hours.'

Ben's face lit with pleasure. 'Is he really?'

Graziella's smile verged on laughter. 'That is what he said.'

'Oh, boy! *When?*'

Graziella checked her watch. 'Eight-thirty.

You have forty-five minutes in which to eat breakfast.'

'And change,' Taylor added, 'be smothered in sunscreen cream and find your sunhat.'

They made it with time to spare, and Taylor sat patiently as Ben hopped from one foot to another, waiting for Dante to appear.

'There he is!'

A very different Dante from the man she was accustomed to seeing, for absent were the sophisticated trappings. Instead, he wore working clothes, well-worn and serviceable, dust-covered boots, with a brimmed hat shading his hard-boned features.

She watched his easy, lithe strides as he drew close, and the sheer physicality of the man caught her breath, a vivid reminder of the strong arms anchoring her body to his as he had kissed her senseless…oh, heavens…eight, nine hours before.

It was all too easy to recall the feel of the possession of his mouth, the size and hardness of his arousal…and the feelings he aroused deep within.

Even now, awareness flared and spread

unbidden through her body, and a part of her ached for the impossible.

How long before he demanded an answer? And what would she say when he did?

For the love of all the patron saints...what *could* she say?

Yes was such a simple word, but the result meant gifting more, so much *more* than she felt equipped to give.

Living, sharing intimacy with a man who simply saw the acquisition of a wife as a convenient solution...despite his denial.

If she did agree, what would that make her? A trophy wife residing in beautiful homes around the world, a generous allowance, a social hostess...content with her husband's presence and attention whenever he chose to give it?

Yet the alternative...could she renege on her sister's wishes? Choose subjecting Ben, in his formative years, to a life of being shuttled between two households on different continents?

And hadn't she already discounted that by agreeing to share Dante's Sydney home? Wasn't that the reason she was here in Tuscany?

But to take the situation a giant leap forward by agreeing to marriage…it was crazy, inconceivable. *Wasn't it?*

'Good morning.'

The sound of Dante's drawled greeting brought Taylor's attention sharply into focus, and she met his musing gaze with equanimity.

'Hi.' Her smile was bright…too bright? Worse, did he divine more than she wanted him to see?

Act, why don't you?

To a degree, wasn't that what she'd been doing since they'd consulted over Ben's welfare in a Sydney legal office…how many weeks ago? Five, six?

'Can we go now?' Ben begged, then he laughed as Dante lifted him high and settled him astride his shoulders.

'I see you're dressed for work,' he teased, and Ben responded with a resounding, 'Yes!'

'In that case, let's go join the men.'

Taylor watched them move down the steps, man and boy, linked by d'Alessandri blood, connected by a loving bond…destined to a future which would bind them together for the rest of their lives.

Lives she would share…completely, or to a lesser degree. The choice was hers.

Enough, already. She had a book to finish, a deadline to meet, and rumination wouldn't achieve pages written.

She glanced towards Graziella, who was in the process of pouring her third espresso, and rose to her feet as Lena came out onto the terrace to clear their table.

'If you'll excuse me, I'll collect my laptop and spend a few hours working.'

'Of course, my dear,' Graziella conceded graciously. 'I'll look forward to seeing you at lunch.'

The library provided the perfect ambience, with its floor-to-ceiling bookcases and large desk, and concentrated effort ensured the necessary focus as Taylor opened her manuscript file, reread the chapter she was currently working on and did some minor editing before creating fresh pages.

Ideal circumstances, the story was in her head…so why didn't the scene flow? The dialogue seemed ho-hum, the narrative sedentary.

All because Dante's forceful image crept insidiously into her mind, and refused to disappear.

After ten minutes, she muttered an unladylike oath, took a deep breath, flexed her fingers…and banished him.

It couldn't be said her fingers flew over the keys, but she achieved a credible number of pages, and frowned when a knock sounded at the thick wooden door, followed by it swinging open to reveal Dante in the aperture.

Taylor looked at him blankly for a few seconds, then realisation hit, and she sank back in the chair.

He'd washed and changed into black jeans and a white chambray shirt with the sleeves rolled back a few turns, showing muscular forearms.

'Lena is about to serve lunch.'

It was one o'clock already? She pressed *save*, closed the laptop and shifted it into one hand. 'Thanks. I'll go tidy up.'

She moved towards the door, pausing when he didn't step aside, and she flicked him a startled glance as he reached out and tucked a wayward lock of hair back behind her ear.

Was she aware of the faint frown that creased her forehead? Hair that looked as if she'd run her fingers through it countless times?

He very much doubted she registered the pulse beating thickly at the base of her throat. It made him want to touch, feel its tempo, then soothe it with his lips.

Instead he offered a lazy smile. 'A productive morning?'

She didn't want to be so conscious of him…the scent of soap, a hint of male essence, the languorous warmth emanating from his powerful body.

'Yes. Thank you,' she added politely, and felt a sense of relief as he moved to one side so she could pass.

Ben waxed lyrical during lunch, a meal comprising pasta, followed by fresh fruit, and eaten in the conservatory.

'The grapes are huge. Dante says they're ripening well.' He looked a little wistful. 'I wish we could stay for the harvest.' His features brightened a slightly. 'Dante says maybe we can next year.'

'You've become his hero,' Taylor accorded quietly as they entered the lobby and began ascending the stairs behind Ben, who was in need of the customary siesta.

'But not yours,' Dante alluded indolently.

She sent him a speaking glance before quickening her steps to reach the upper level, and she deliberately refrained from casting him a further glance as she accompanied Ben to their guest wing.

While Ben napped, she settled cross-legged on her bed and opened her laptop, working until Ben woke, after which they checked on the mother cat and her kittens, then together they played handball, throwing and dribbling it, laughing as one of the dogs decided to join in the game.

It was there Dante found them, and he stood watching for a few minutes, a smile curving his mouth as Taylor called 'not fair' when Ben threw the ball high, and she laughed as he scrambled to get to it before she did.

'Foul!' This from Ben, when she snagged the ball, turned and ran with it…and hit a solid mass.

Human, she registered as hands took hold of her shoulders and steadied her.

There was a brief moment when the breath huffed from her body, an apology escaping her lips, then she stilled as she realised who held her.

Ben raced forward to join them. 'Dante! Are you going to play ball with me and Taylor?'

'Two against one?' Dante posed. 'I think I can manage that.'

He did, admirably, but he also let them win, and Ben punched the air as the score tipped by one point in his and Taylor's favour.

'Game over,' Taylor called as she reached for the band holding her hair, automatically pulling it free before bunching the length together and deftly tying it back into a pony-tail.

Dante hadn't even broken a sweat, Taylor perceived as he ruffled Ben's hair.

'Go indoors and have a cool drink,' he bade with a smile. 'I'll see you at dinner.'

'If Taylor comes with me, can I have a swim in the pool?'

'Of course. But only if Taylor is with you.'

'I know,' Ben reassured happily.

It made for a pleasant end to the afternoon, as Ben proudly displayed his swimming prowess in the large pool beneath its enclosure of tinted glass.

Afterwards they showered separately in the ad-

joining bathing room, then, dressed, they retreated upstairs to view television until it was
time to change and go down for dinner.

CHAPTER NINE

THAT day set a precedent for the days which followed.

Dante took Ben with him each morning, while Taylor set up her laptop in the library. Mostly, she extended her writing while Ben rested after lunch, and their afternoons were spent at play, swimming, together with an hour in Graziella's company as she taught her grandson the rudiments of the Italian language.

There was nothing to pre-warn more than a week after their arrival at the villa that the day would prove any different from the ones preceding it.

It was an urgent call during lunch for Graziella which absented her from the table for several minutes, and she returned displaying visible distress.

Dante rose to his feet at once. 'There's a problem?'

'My sister Bianca,' Graziella relayed with concern, 'has been admitted to hospital, and is scheduled to have surgery late this afternoon.' She cast him a look of despair. 'I must go to her.'

'Of course,' he agreed at once. 'I'll have Lena help you pack, then I'll drive you home.' He pressed his lips to her forehead. 'But first, finish your lunch.'

Except it seemed beyond her, and Taylor felt the need to ask, 'Is there anything I can do?'

Graziella shook her head. 'No, my dear. Thank you.' She leant forward and pressed a hand to Ben's shoulder. 'We'll see each other soon. A few days, perhaps.'

'*Sì*, Nonna.'

A faint smile curved her lips. '*Bravo*,' she complimented. 'Now, if you'll excuse me?'

Fifteen minutes later Taylor and Ben stood at the front entrance and waved as the four-wheel-drive eased away from the courtyard with Dante at the wheel.

Dinner was a quiet meal shared only with Ben,

followed later by his bedtime story. Taylor waited until he fell asleep before she retrieved her laptop and retreated to the library for a few hours.

Too many, she recognised close to midnight as she lifted her arms high in a stretch meant to ease the tension in her shoulders.

She dared not risk more coffee, or she'd be too wired to sleep…but a further half-hour should enable her to piece together the current scene, then she'd go to bed.

The internal lighting throughout the hallways had dimmed down via automatic timer when Taylor emerged from the library, and her steps faltered as she entered the main lobby and saw Dante cross towards the stairs.

He caught sight of her, and paused, waiting for her to join him, and her grip on the laptop tightened involuntarily as she drew close.

'Working late?'

She looked tired, her eyes too large in her face, and her hair looked as if she'd run fingers through it on a regular basis.

'Yes.'

Her voice sounded slightly husky, and he had

the sudden urge to ease the faint frown from her forehead, sweep back the hair from her face and turn the slight wariness there into something else.

Beneath the surface of her control there was passion...and existent was a desire to break the ice encasing her emotions, to stoke the heat to fire. For the fire existed, he was sure.

Experience, honed and refined, had taught him that strategy brought the prize. He just needed to exert patience, and he had that.

Yet there was knowledge that if he followed his instincts, he'd lift her into his arms and carry her to bed. *His*. Undress her, then make slow leisurely love until she was consumed by passion, body and soul. Cradle her close and hold her through what remained of the night...then stir her into an erotic waking at first light.

Instead, he'd be content with less...for now.

'Graziella?' Taylor queried with polite interest, and the need to say something, *anything* to dispel the emotional tension that seemed to encapsulate them both.

'Her sister's surgery is successful, and Bianca is expected to fully recover.'

'I'm glad,' she said simply. *Go*, a tiny voice silently urged. *Now.* Except she stood still, momentarily unable to move.

Then it was too late as he framed her face with his hands and brushed his lips against her own, then he deepened the kiss until a groan of protest sounded in her throat had him easing back.

For a long moment Taylor could only look at him, unaware of the tremulous movement of her slightly swollen mouth, the stark darkness in her eyes.

His lips curved a little in a soft smile as he gently relinquished his hands from her face. 'Go to bed,' he bade quietly, 'before I'm tempted to take you to mine.'

Shock, and something else, was a fleeting, barely evident emotion, then it was gone, as without a further word she moved round him and quickly ascended the stairs, her breathing only settling upon reaching the sanctuary of her suite.

Graziella's absence from the villa became more noticeable at mealtimes, when her presence provided a welcome buffer in more ways than one.

Ben didn't appear to notice Taylor's marked

effort to slip easily into innocuous conversation during lunch and dinner. Breakfast proved a breeze, as she shared the meal with Ben out on the terrace each morning, then when Dante came up from the fields to fetch Ben she habitually collected a second cup of coffee in one hand, her laptop in the other, and retreated to work in the library.

Soon their sojourn at the villa would end, and they'd return to Graziella's apartment in Florence. Preceding, inevitably, their flight to Sydney.

There was a part of her that missed the familiar...especially the opportunity to meet Sheyna for coffee and a chat.

Yet there was something about the villa and vineyard which pulled at her emotions, knowing she would feel a little sad to leave... and pleased whenever Dante suggested they return.

Which brought the future vividly to mind...a subject Dante broached a few evenings later as they emerged from Ben's room after settling him to sleep.

'Shall we head down to the library?'

Taylor spared him a glance. 'Together?'

He offered her a slow smile. 'Is that a problem?'

Yes. 'No, of course not.'

They reached the head of the stairs and began to descend.

'Ben is fine,' she endorsed with genuine pleasure, and a wide smile curved her generous mouth. 'It's been wonderful for him here.'

'I agree.'

He opened the library door and ushered her inside, then he crossed to the desk, leant one hip against its edge and fixed her with an unwavering scrutiny.

'There are certain legalities required for a civil marriage ceremony in Italy.' His voice was quiet, almost silky, and she felt her heart leap into her throat.

She lifted a hand in a silent entreaty to *stop*...looking at him carefully, noting the leashed strength apparent, eyes that were dark, almost still as she met and held his gaze.

'I don't recall *agreeing* to marriage.'

'You would be content with a relationship without the formality of a marriage certificate?'

'We don't have a *relationship*.'

'What would you call it, Taylor?' He paused, then went in for the kill. 'You think I don't know how you react in my arms when I kiss you? That I can't sense your body tremble beneath my touch? Feel the rapid beat of your heart? *Know*,' he reiterated quietly, 'that you, as I do, need the fulfilment of sexual intimacy.'

She swore she stopped breathing, then her body's natural mechanism forced her to gulp in air.

'So…what is it to be? The furtive or open sharing of a bed? Or do we legalise the union?'

It wasn't as if the whole *marriage* thing hadn't consumed her mind during waking hours and intruded into her dreams from the moment he'd introduced the subject. 'I don't want to sleep with you.'

'*Sleep* being a euphemism for sex?' There was a glimmer of humour existent in his voice. 'You want me to disprove that statement?'

She had no doubt he could, all too easily, up to a certain point.

The pertinent question being whether *she* could relax sufficiently to overcome the underlying fear that had remained with her for almost two years.

Better to tell him *now*, she rationalised, than say nothing and freeze up at the inappropriate moment…or worse.

'There's something you should know.' She closed her eyes, then opened them again. A slight hysterical sound threatened to emerge, and she bit it back…caught the darkness in his eyes, then she lifted her head a little and held his gaze.

'I have an issue with intimacy.' There, she'd said it. She took in a deep breath, then followed with the basic facts of her assault and kept it brief. Very brief.

Dante's expression didn't change, but anger simmered beneath the surface as he recalled vividly the night she'd cried out in the throes of a nightmare. A nightmare which obviously had its base in reality.

'How badly were you hurt?'

Scars, she had a few of those, faded now. Fractured ribs, a fractured hip, two fractured fingers. Taylor managed a light shrug. 'I survived.'

He watched the fleeting emotions chase across

her features, glimpsed the faint edge of remembered pain. 'Were you hospitalised?'

His voice was surprisingly gentle, and it made her want to cry. Something she refused to do in his presence.

'Yes,' she managed.

The thought of the physical and emotional trauma she must have suffered almost undid him. 'Why didn't I hear about it?'

She held his gaze, and she didn't look away. 'Leon was overseas,' she said quietly. 'And I swore Casey to secrecy.' She held his gaze, and pre-empted the question she was certain he'd ask. 'And the answer is *no*. I wasn't raped.'

But close enough, Dante deduced, to leave emotional scars and a distrust of allowing a man to get too close.

He eased his body upright and closed the distance between them. Then he captured her chin between thumb and forefinger and tilted it so she had to look at him.

'You misjudge me if you think it makes any difference.' He soothed a path over her lower lip with his thumb.

Taylor wasn't capable of saying a word, nor was she conscious of the way her mouth trembled beneath his touch.

'I need some time,' she managed at last, and her eyes widened as he shook his head.

'Time isn't going to change anything,' Dante offered quietly, and caught the faint shadow of concern deepen the green flecks in her eyes.

'But why *here*?'

'Graziella. We owe it to her, don't you agree?'

'Dante—'

'*Cara*, the only word I'll accept is *yes*.' He grazed her lips with his own. 'Say it.'

She did, with a degree of helpless fatalism.

There was nothing *simple* about a private wedding ceremony, Taylor soon learned, as Dante put the wheels in motion to expedite the completion and filing of the necessary paperwork required to gain their marriage licence.

Telling Ben resulted in an excited and positive response, which did much to ease Taylor's mind.

While Dante dealt quietly, but firmly, with Graziella, who insisted the wedding be held in a favoured church in Florence...and who conceded a private civil ceremony held at the vineyard was more appropriate given the recent tragic loss of two beloved family members.

The few guests would be limited to immediate family and the staff who worked at the vineyard, and Bruno and Mariangela would undertake the catering.

There was, however, a day spent in Florence with Graziella, searching for *the* perfect outfit Taylor should wear on *the* day.

Ivory silk, cunningly cut to skim her slender curves before falling gracefully to her ankles, a lovely scooped neckline and sleeveless, it came with a delicate ivory lace bolero with slim-fitting full-length sleeves.

Perfect, Taylor declared, adding ivory satin stiletto pumps to complete the outfit...and, to appease Graziella, a gorgeous, understated head-piece with a fingertip veil edged in matching ivory lace.

'You will wear my pearls,' Graziella stated. 'They'll add the final touch.'

A visit to the hallowed sanctum of a prominent

jeweller featured on their to-do list, who, on advance instructions from Dante, carefully examined Taylor's hand, then he measured her ring finger and made several notations before assuring the rings, plural, would be despatched to Signor d'Alessandri in person.

Dante, who, after depositing Graziella and Taylor in one of the most fashionable areas in the city, took Ben to visit a museum, then met with them at a prearranged restaurant for dinner.

He arrived first with Ben, and moved forward to greet them as they entered the foyer, brushing his lips to Taylor's cheek, then Graziella's, and viewed the many designer-emblazoned packages of varying sizes which both women carried in both hands.

He consigned the packages into the *maître d*'s care, who in turn summoned a waiter to take them to their table.

'You've had a successful day?'

'*Sì*,' Graziella agreed with enthusiasm. 'Although you will need to tell Taylor, as a d'Alessandri she must allow her husband to pay for her clothes, and anything else she chooses to purchase.'

Dante offered Taylor a quizzical look, which she returned in kind.

'I have my own money.' It was a quiet, but firm averral, and one which she intended to enforce, despite Dante handing her a card attached to his own account and instructing her to use it.

The wine steward presented a bottle of champagne, skilfully released the cork, then ceremoniously filled their flutes, and poured lemonade for Ben.

Menus were presented, their orders placed, and the food was divine. The conversation didn't lag, although it became apparent as the evening progressed that Graziella was beginning to visibly tire.

It was almost eleven when they delivered Graziella to her apartment, taking coffee she insisted on serving them before leaving for the drive back to the vineyard.

Dante slid a CD into the console player as they headed south from the city, and Taylor leant back against the head-rest, closed her eyes and let the music soothe her senses. Ben sat slumped in sleep in his booster seat.

In less than forty-eight hours she'd become Taylor *d'Alessandri*, Dante's wife. Within a week of the marriage, together with Ben, they'd return to Sydney and life would revert to normal.

A faint sigh whispered from her lips as she conjugated *normal*.

She must have dozed, for she became conscious the four-wheel-drive was stationary outside the main entrance to the villa and Dante was no longer at the wheel. When she checked the back seat, Ben was no longer there.

Taylor released the door ready to alight as he emerged from the lobby, and he took in her shoeless feet and swept her into his arms.

'Hey, I can walk,' she protested as he carried her indoors and set the alarm as he locked up. Her collection of shopping bags was located atop a long credenza, and she smiled with remembered pleasure as Dante moved to the stairs and began to ascend them.

'Put me down.'

'Soon.'

The solid beat of his heart against her ribs ratcheted up her breathing, and the faint aroma of his cologne teased her senses, bringing them into pulsating life.

She had the sudden urge to press her lips to the curve of his neck, nip a little, then soothe the mark with her tongue.

Except if she did it would be tantamount to an invitation, and she swayed a little as he set her down onto her feet outside the door to Ben's room.

A quick look at the childish form curled beneath the bedclothes was sufficient to see all was well, and she preceded Dante into the hallway to hover outside her suite.

She opened her mouth to wish him 'goodnight', only to have the word locked in her throat as he gathered her in and took possession of her mouth in a kiss that rocked her soul.

There was an awareness of being caught up in a whirlpool, and she held on, giving herself over to the spellbinding sensuality of his touch.

Then he eased back, gentling the pressure of his mouth, until it became a light brush of lips on her own.

At last he lifted his head, and his eyes were dark, so dark they were almost black.

'Invite me in, or tell me to leave.'

She wanted him to ease the ache vibrating deep inside, and she'd have given anything to open the door and pull him inside. To slip the buttons free on his shirt, unbuckle the belt at his waist and dispense with her own clothing in the need to feel the heat, the passion of fulfilment only he could give her.

Her eyes seared his, dark and incredibly poignant. She felt her lips tremble, yet no words emerged past the sudden lump that had risen in her throat.

For a moment something flared in the depths of his eyes, then it was gone, and he gently eased her to arm's length, leant in and brushed his mouth to her forehead.

Then he turned and traversed the wide hallway to his suite on the opposite side of the villa.

CHAPTER TEN

THE day of the wedding began much as the days before it, with breakfast eaten out on the terrace with Ben and Graziella, whom Dante had collected from Florence the previous evening.

A stunning gazebo stood on the manicured lawn adjacent the villa itself, and a florist was due any time soon with suitable floral decorations.

It had become impossible to prevent Graziella putting a romantic spin on *the day*. Especially when Dante's mother had to know the marriage wasn't a love match.

At least, not in the accepted sense, Taylor reflected as she sought to still the nerves fluttering inside her stomach.

The ceremony was timed for six, followed by drinks, dinner, after which the newly married couple would spend the weekend in a luxury hotel in Florence, while Graziella remained at the villa to care for Ben.

As the day progressed, so did the volume of activity both indoors and outdoors, as carpet was unrolled to form a path to the flower-festooned gazebo. Chairs were set out on the grass, and redolent aromas drifted from the vicinity of the kitchen as Mariangela and Bruno prepared food, while staff set up the terrace for the reception.

Fortunately the events leading up to the ceremony itself left Taylor little time to *think*... and when she *did*, she forced herself to rational-ise marrying Dante was a sensible option.

However, no amount of logic helped soothe the nervous tension escalating throughout her body.

By the time she retreated to her suite to prepare for the ceremony, she was a mess. A shower helped, and she stood beneath the hot-water spray much longer than necessary before emerging to towel herself dry, then begin to dress.

Twice she needed to wipe her mouth clean of lipstick and begin again, and, although the dress slipped on without a hitch, her fingers shook so much she had to reposition and pin her headpiece more than once.

Then Ben was there, ready to escort her downstairs, and she cast him a warm smile.

'You look like a princess.'

His compliment held a degree of awe, and she hugged him close. 'And you must be the handsome prince.' She tucked his hand in hers.

'Dante gave me the rings,' Ben revealed solemnly. 'They're in my pocket.'

'In that case, we should get on with the wedding.'

Together they descended the staircase to the foyer, where Graziella waited for them.

'You're quite breathtakingly lovely, my dear,' Graziella complimented graciously, and, leaning forward, she clasped Taylor's hands. 'I know you'll be very happy.'

'Thank you.' Did Graziella have any idea how much it cost to conquer her nerves and walk the carpeted path to where Dante stood at the flower-festooned gazebo?

To smile and *pretend*?

She was barely conscious of the soft background

music emitting from hidden speakers as Graziella and Ben flanked her, setting a slow pace.

There were guests seated on either side of the carpet, but she saw only the stunningly attractive man who turned to watch her progress.

On some level she recognised the strength apparent beneath the elegance, the aura of power evident in his hard-boned facial features.

His generous mouth curved into a warm smile as she drew close, and her own parted a little as he took hold of her hand and lifted it to his lips.

'Grazie.'

She couldn't stop the way her mouth trembled as he lightly brushed his thumb across the throbbing veins at her wrist.

He didn't release her hand, merely threaded his fingers through her own as they turned towards the celebrant.

It was a simple ceremony, with vows offered and acceded to, the exchange of rings, followed by the announcement Dante and Taylor were now man and wife.

He surprised her by lifting her left hand and pressing his lips to her wedding ring, then amid voiced 'congratulations' he drew her close and kissed her.

A little too thoroughly for her comfort, and colour pinked her cheeks as he released his hold.

Together they walked the carpet, pausing to accept good wishes, then the guests followed them onto the terrace, where champagne flowed and good wishes were offered in abundance.

Taylor smiled as Dante hoisted Ben onto his shoulders, and held him there for a while before letting him slide down to play with some of the children present, young sons and daughters of staff who worked the vineyard.

There was a sense of unreality as she glanced at the wide diamond-encrusted band circling the appropriate finger of her left hand. It was, without doubt, magnificent.

Dante never moved far from her side, while Graziella moved graciously among the guests and kept an eye on the children.

Then it was time to be seated, as Mariangela and Bruno served the food…*gnocchi* in a delicate cream and mushroom sauce, followed by chicken portions roasted in white wine with rosemary, accompanied by a variety of sautéed vegetables. There was a tangy lemon sorbet, a superb tiramisu…and a beautifully decorated wedding cake.

Champagne and wine flowed, and afterwards the tables were cleared to one side, CDs were played on an electronic system and there was dancing.

The overhead lights dimmed a little, and Taylor was conscious of the sensual thrall as Dante drew her close in against him.

All too soon it was time to bid their guests 'goodnight' and settle a weary Ben into bed with a kiss and the ritual 'love you, sleep tight'.

'I won't be long,' Taylor said quietly as Dante opened the door to her suite and followed her in.

Her bag was packed, awaiting only the inclusion of a few last-minute items, and the clothes she'd selected to wear to the hotel rested on a hanger within easy reach.

'Do you need any help?'

'I can manage,' she assured quickly on a slightly strangled note as she retrieved the hanger and moved into the *en suite*.

The headdress came first, followed by the lace bolero, Graziella's pearls, then she released the zip fastener and slipped out of her wedding dress.

Within minutes she donned the classic-styled evening trouser suit in deep emerald-green, slid her feet into elegant stilettos, retouched her lipstick, then she emerged into the bedroom and slipped the final few things into her bag.

'Ready?'

Taylor flicked him a nervous glance, and forced herself to smile. 'Yes.' Blinked, as he cupped her cheek for a brief instant before he collected her bag and indicated she precede him from the suite.

The drive into the city seemed alternately long, yet too short…a contradiction in terms, if ever there was one, and her nervous tension increased measurably as Dante slid the four-wheel-drive into the forecourt of their hotel.

Situated in a quiet enclave, it held Florentine charm with a Tuscan-style *loggia*, and even at this late hour they were greeted by the concierge, their bags retrieved and the four-wheel-drive dispensed for valet parking.

Check-in was a mere formality, and they were directed to a beautifully presented luxury suite, softly lit in welcome.

Then the door slid shut with a refined click…and they were alone.

She was conscious of Dante's appraisal as he shrugged off his jacket, then he removed his tie and unbuttoned the top buttons of his shirt.

'Why don't you make yourself comfortable?'

Sure, and *comfortable* was a state she'd achieve any time soon?

Did she know she resembled a startled doe caught in a vehicle's headlights, momentarily powerless to move?

Dante held her gaze, and glimpsed the sudden stillness in her stance, the slight, almost imperceptible lift of her chin as she watched him cross to her side. Sensed the slight hitch in her breathing as he reached for the pins holding her hair in its smooth twist, dealt with them all, then threaded his fingers through the silky length and tucked a wayward swathe behind her ear.

'Why don't you change, put on a robe, and we'll relax for a while?'

It was after midnight, and all she wanted to do was shed her clothes, crawl beneath the bedcovers…and sleep. However, there was only one bed…granted, it was king-sized, but the thought of sharing it with him sent her into a state of emotional chaos.

So…suck it up, a tiny voice taunted. You agreed to this marriage and all it involves. Tonight…tomorrow. *Hell*, next *week*…what's the difference?

Maybe a hot shower might help soothe her nerves a little, and she crossed to her bag, removed a sleep T-shirt and cotton sleep trousers, collected toiletries and moved into the *en suite*.

Bliss, absolute bliss, Taylor conceded as she stepped beneath the spray of water. Hot, she needed it hot, and she adjusted the dial and let the water cascade down her back.

Rose-scented soap emitted a delicate perfume, and she closed her eyes as she smoothed it over her shoulders, then moved to her nape.

A slight sound close by had her eyes flying open, only to widen with shocked surprise as Dante stepped into the shower cubicle.

'You can't—' Her voice faltered as he calmly took the soap from her hand and stepped behind her. Seconds later soap skimmed her shoulders and moved steadily down her back. *Do this*, she finished silently.

Except it appeared he had every intention of remaining, and she arched forward as he shaped her bottom, lingered there, then he gently turned her round to face him.

She was tall, even in bare feet, but he stood a head above her, and she tilted her chin a little to meet his faintly hooded gaze. 'What do you think you're doing?'

Was that her voice? It sounded impossibly husky, even faintly choking.

'Bathing you.'

'I'm quite capable,' she protested, and sought to take the soap from him, only to fail miserably.

'I'm not done yet.'

'Please—' The plea emerged as a strangled gasp as he stroked soap over one breast, shaped it…then rendered a similar treatment to its twin, before moving to her waist, her stomach.

'Stop right there,' she managed as he reached

the soft hair curling at the apex of her thighs, and she gave a compulsive jerk as he moved low, palming the soap as he sought the sensitive clitoris with unerring accuracy.

Taylor bucked as sensation arrowed from deep within, radiating through her body, and an unbidden cry emerged from her lips as he intensified his touch.

Anything further she might have uttered was lost as he took possession of her mouth in a kiss that tore the breath from her throat and sensation spiralled beyond her control in a shattering climax so intense her body shook with it.

Dante slowly relinquished her mouth, his eyes dark and slumberous as he took in her dazed expression, dilated eyes that seemed too large for her face, and something stirred inside him, prompting an involuntary thought…which he instantly dismissed.

With a slight smile he placed the soap in her hand.

'Your turn.'

You have to be kidding.

'I don't think—'

He cupped her hand in his own and transferred it to his chest. 'It's simple.'

For him, maybe. Except for her it rapidly became something incredibly seductive as he guided her hand in a thorough exploration of his body, before presenting her with his back.

Was he aware her hand shook a little as she lathered hard musculature at his shoulders, his taut ribcage, tapered waist and tight butt?

She fervently hoped not.

He turned to face her, and passion shimmered from every pore...hot, deep and dark. On one level it frightened her...yet on another, she was held fascinated.

Then he lowered his head and captured her mouth, using his tongue to stroke her own, to plunder and savour as he enticed her response.

Just as it became almost too intense to handle, he lifted her high and slid her down onto his hardened length, absorbing her startled cry as he surged deep...only to experience shock when he sensed delicate membrane tear as he sank in to the hilt.

He stilled and, lifting his mouth from her

own, he swore softly. *'Madre di Dio*. Why didn't you tell me?'

His eyes were dark, so dark she felt almost afraid. 'Would you have believed me if I had?'

Per meraviglia. Dante closed his eyes, then opened them again. 'I'd have ensured more care.' A longer, gentler initiation, for a start.

She attempted a light shrug, conscious only of a slight stinging sensation as he carefully lifted her free of him...heard him utter something almost beneath his breath, and knew she wouldn't care for the translation.

He handed her the soap, and when she was done he used it on himself, then closed the water dial, filched a towel and wound it round his hips, before reaching for another.

Taylor held out her hand for it, and opened her mouth to protest as he began blotting the moisture from her body.

'I don't need for you to...' she began, and left the remaining words unsaid beneath his intense look.

Minutes later she gasped as he swept her into his arms and carried her into the bedroom.

'What are you doing?'

'Taking you to bed.' He thrust back the covers and drew her down onto the mattress with him.

'Dante—'

'Trust me,' he said gently, and lowered his head to fasten his mouth on her own in a kiss filled with languorous warmth as he teased and tasted until he felt her unbidden response.

Somehow her towel no longer offered a shield, and he trailed light, feathery kisses over her cheek to nuzzle the sensitive pulse beneath her ear, before tracing a path to the curve of her neck, lingered there…and sensed, rather than heard, the soft, almost inaudible groan in her throat.

His hand moved to cup her breast, and she gasped as he took the peak beneath thumb and forefinger and rolled it…before rendering a similar salutation to its twin.

Then he moved, savouring the soft fullness with his lips, nipping lightly until he reached the tautened peak, and she cried out as he took it in his mouth and suckled until she arched beneath his touch.

In a tortuously slow supplication he shifted his head and inched up the sensation with ease, aware of the way she restlessly moved her head from side to side before reaching out to clutch hold of his shoulders.

Not content, he slid low, tracing a path to her navel, lingering there, before trailing over her stomach to the soft, soap-scented hair curling into a V near the juncture of her thighs.

Taylor drew in a sharp breath and reached for his head as he moved lower, almost crying out loud as he sought and found the slightly swollen bud.

Surely he wouldn't…but he did, laving it gently as it throbbed into vibrant life, and she bucked beneath the onslaught, unable to control the wildly curling sensation spiralling deep within.

It rose, increasing in tempo until she almost screamed as he drove her high…higher than she imagined it was possible to go, only to send her further, and he held her as she shattered.

He barely let her catch her breath before he sent her up again, using his wicked mouth in an intimate kiss that made her beg in a voice she didn't recognise as her own, only that she desperately needed *more*…and she reached for him as he moved over her and held on as he eased his turgid length into her moist heat.

'Look at me. Only me,' Dante commanded gently, and he groaned as her vaginal muscles sheathed him…saw her expression of wonder as he eased in, rested there, then he began to move.

Her eyes went dark as she caught his rhythm, instinctively matching it, and he saw the moment she began the passionate spiral towards the brink, taking him with her as they climaxed together in an emotional orgasm so intensely acute, it was almost more than she could bear.

It seemed an age before the flood of sensation began to subside, and she didn't protest as he reached for the bedcovers…or when he gathered her in close against him.

There wasn't a word that came readily to mind to describe what she'd just experienced. Only intense joy and a feeling of complete fulfilment. Boneless, she added, knowing nothing came close.

'Thank you.'

She felt the touch of his lips against her temple.

'You're welcome.'

Taylor shifted her hand until it lay over his

heart, and the steady beat soothed her into a state of dreamless inertia, summoning sleep.

Taylor woke to the tantalising aroma of freshly brewed coffee, and she stretched, felt the unaccustomed pull of unused muscles combining with a delicious aching sensation deep inside, opened her eyes, glimpsed the unfamiliar suite... and remembered.

'Good morning.'

She looked at the tall male robed figure standing in the aperture between the bedroom and adjoining lounge area, and stifled a yawn at the sound of Dante's musing drawl.

'Back at you,' she managed, and pushed aside the bedcovers, only to pull them back again with the discovery she was wearing *zilch*. She had a robe somewhere...

'Is this what you're looking for?'

She took the robe he held out to her, and shrugged into it with as much decency as she could muster.

'Modesty, Taylor?' he teased, delighting in the soft pink colouring her cheeks. 'When I've seen and tasted every inch of you?'

Yes, well… She spared him a telling glance. 'I don't possess your degree of *laissez-faire*.'

His husky laughter curled round her heart-strings and pulled a little. 'Come join me for coffee. Breakfast will be here soon.' He reached out a hand, and she took it, felt the warm clasp as he tugged her to her feet.

'You slept well.'

It wasn't a question, and she inclined her head in silent acquiescence. How could she not, when her body still sang from his touch?

Sex, she viewed logically, then qualified…*very* good sex, was one of nature's aphrodisiacs.

Taylor moved into the *en suite*, completed her usual morning routine, caught the length of her hair into a pony-tail, then emerged to find a waiter transferring covered dishes onto the table.

It smelled divine, and she lifted covers as Dante signed the chit, sighing with pleasure as she saw the contents, and she settled comfortably in a chair.

Coffee, juice, a savoury mushroom omelette, thick slabs of toasted ciabatta bread, jams, fruit…it was a veritable feast.

'Do you have any plans for the day?'

Dante took the chair opposite, and she quelled the sensation arrowing through her body at the sight of him. There was something vaguely primitive about him, the hard-planed features, and a mouth to die for.

Even *thinking* about that mouth and what it had wickedly achieved sent the blood racing through her veins.

Did he have any idea how he affected her?

Possibly…remembering her reaction to his touch.

At that moment he caught her gaze, glimpsed the thudding pulse at the base of her throat, the way she lifted her hand to instinctively hide it, and his lips curved into a smile.

'What would you like to do?'

There were a few gifts she'd like to buy to take home to friends, and it would be nice just to wander and browse, pause for a *gelato*, maybe coffee. Enjoy lunch somewhere.

'The San Lorenzo market?'

'You want to play tourist?'

'Would you mind?'

It would be something of a novelty. He couldn't recall any of his female companions choosing the markets over exclusive boutiques.

He offered her a gleaming glance, and indicated breakfast. 'Eat, then we'll make an early start.'

It was almost ten when they emerged from the hotel into stunningly warm sunshine, and Taylor viewed the day ahead with a lightened heart.

Did it matter so much her marriage wasn't a love match?

Don't go there, a tiny voice advised.

Live for the day. Wasn't that life's sage motto? It was certainly one she intended to observe.

Dante found the market shopping experience fascinating. At least, Taylor's approach to it brought an amused smile to his lips from time to time, as she browsed, examined, discarded…repeating the process until she found an item which appealed, whereupon her bargaining skills came into play.

He observed as vendors conversant in the English language gestured helplessly and pretended not to understand.

Taylor watched as Dante intervened, and she

watched the visible change in the vendor's demeanour as he handed over the item in exchange for euros.

'Thank you.' She opened her wallet. 'How much do I owe you?'

'Consider it a gift.'

She looked at him carefully, shook her head, and attempted to push notes into his hand.

A gesture which resulted in an eyebrow slanting in mocking cynicism. 'You want to argue?'

'Not particularly.'

'Then don't.'

A fellow tourist moved a little too close, jostling her, and Dante slid a protective arm along the back of her waist.

For someone who knew women, how their minds worked and the various ploys they employed in numerous guises...Taylor's fierce independence amused him.

Any other woman of his acquaintance would expect him to pick up the tab for anything that took her whim...most often angle prettily for an expensive item.

Dante chose a small café for lunch, after

which Taylor added to her purchases, and they walked, lingering in front of a church and some fine old buildings as he imparted their historical background.

It was a pleasant day, one she would hold close to her heart, and she didn't protest when he indicated they return to their hotel as early evening began to descend.

'I've booked a table for dinner at the hotel restaurant,' Dante relayed as they entered their suite. 'We'll shower and change, then go down to the bar for a drink.'

Taylor turned towards him with a smile. 'That'll be nice.' And looked at him in silent askance as he reached for her, angling his mouth over hers in a kiss that sent the blood fizzing in her veins.

Piercingly sweet, it held leashed restraint as he curved an arm down her back and pulled her in close.

She was conscious of an electric, pulsing ache deep inside, and she wound her arms round his neck and kissed him back, exulting in the wild almost pagan need that held her body in thrall.

He framed her face, tilting it, and used his

thumbs to caress each side of her jaw before sliding his hands down to shape her shoulders, lingered a little, then he moved to cup her breasts, lightly fingering their tender peaks...and saw her eyes glaze.

With one easy movement he slipped his hands beneath the light top she wore, dispensed with it, then he released the clasp of her bra.

She was beautiful, her slender curves revealing admirable symmetry, and he skimmed her ribs...felt then, rather than saw, the faint, thickened scar, and comprehension flared as he traced it with a gentle finger.

Taylor lifted a hand in a defensive gesture, then let it drop as his eyes seared her own...dark, dangerous in their intensity.

'Your assailant kicked you?' A muscle bunched at the edge of his jaw as he imagined the impact. Enough, Dante recognised grimly, to ensure she'd suffered agonising pain. 'Taylor?'

She closed her eyes as he brushed his lips to her temple. 'More than once?'

'Yes.'

'The police caught and arrested him?'

He'd attacked her in a rage at being disturbed, then fled, disappearing from the house into the dark of night. 'No.'

'You saw his face?'

It would remain indelibly etched in her mind, and an involuntary shiver shook her slim form as the image appeared in stark relief. 'Yes.'

'*Santo cielo.*' The imprecation was barely audible as he enfolded her close.

She wasn't sure how long he held her, only that he did, and after a few long minutes she lifted her head, saw the darkness in his eyes, and her mouth curved into a smile.

'How come I'm almost naked, and you're not?' she managed lightly, and caught his faint smile as he let her move to arm's length.

'Be my guest.'

Undress him? He had to be kidding.

'I don't think that's a good idea.'

'Pity.' He lifted a hand and pressed a finger to her lower lip. 'We could always order in.'

'And miss playing dress-up and mingling with fellow guests?' She moved away, then looked back over one shoulder. 'See you in ten.'

He was tempted to follow her, and almost did. Except his mobile rang, and he checked caller ID, saw it was an international call and took it, responding in rapid French before ending the communication.

Dante thrust a hand into his trouser pocket and crossed to the window. A problem requiring his personal attention, and one which would involve flying to Paris on Tuesday to attend a meeting.

He entered the *en suite* as Taylor stepped out from the shower cubicle, and he arched an eyebrow as she quickly reached for a towel and wound it round her damp form.

It was interesting to see how easily she became flustered on occasion. Most women of his acquaintance would reveal rather than conceal, and delight in providing provocation.

Something primitive stirred deep inside, and he shot her a teasing glance as he discarded his robe.

'You could always wash my back.'

'I don't think it's your back you have in mind.'

His husky laughter brought swift colour to her cheeks as she averted her eyes from his splendid, very naked body.

Except he reached out, caught hold of her chin and dropped a brief, hard kiss on her mouth. 'Don't ever change, *cara*.'

Then he stepped into the shower cubicle, turned on the water dial and began spreading soap over his chest without casting her so much as another glance.

Taylor gathered up the clothes she'd worn and retreated into the bedroom to don underwear, then she dressed in a stunning black evening trouser suit, slid her feet into stilettos, fastened a diamond pendant at her nape, added matching earrings, and slid on a wide gold bracelet that had belonged to her mother.

Make-up didn't take long, just a light moisturiser, a light dusting of bronze powder, lipstick and a touch of eye-shadow and mascara.

She was about to twist her hair into a careless knot atop her head when Dante emerged into the room and began pulling on trousers.

Taylor met his gaze via mirrored reflection, watching as he shrugged into the shirt and began tending to the buttons.

It took mere minutes to fix her hair and fasten

the knot in place with a strategically placed clasp, then she gathered up an evening bag, checked the contents and preceded him from their suite.

The restaurant immediately adjoined the hotel and resembled a large conservatory built in panelled tinted glass.

Definitely *wow* factor, Taylor silently accorded, noting the gleaming marble floor, tables set with white linen and bracketed by comfortable leather chairs.

The *maître d'* greeted them with due reverence reserved for the élite, then personally led them to their table and saw them seated.

One flick of his fingers, and a wine steward appeared and solicitously enquired Dante's choice.

'You've been here before.' Taylor sent him a musing smile as the wine steward disappeared.

'Occasionally.'

A waiter presented two beautiful leather embossed menus, made a few suggestions before retreating to tend guests at another table.

Taylor chose a starter, followed it with another as a main and declined dessert, while Dante elected for a starter, a pasta dish, and selected a platter of cheeses and fruit.

The wine, the food…both were superb, and it was pleasant to enjoy the excellent service, the ambience.

It provided a lovely way in which to end the day, and she said as much as Dante signed the bill.

'My pleasure.'

Just the thought of the touch of his mouth on hers brought her body alive, and she longed for the confidence to seek his possession, to tease, tantalise and entice his response. Drive him wild…and have him reciprocate.

Instead, she walked at his side in companionable silence, preceded him into their suite, and proceeded to undress, remove her make-up and the clasp from her hair.

Then she pulled on her sleep top, secured her cotton sleep trousers, and slid beneath the bed-covers to join the man who rested at arm's length beside her.

Seconds later he extinguished the bed-side lamp and the room was plunged into darkness.

Then she felt him move and he gathered her in

against him, and nestled her head into the curve of his shoulder.

It was early dawn when he teased her into wakefulness, then made slow, evocative love with such gentleness it almost brought her undone.

CHAPTER ELEVEN

IT WAS late afternoon when the four-wheel-drive drew to a halt in front of the Montepulciano villa, and almost as soon as Dante switched off the engine the front door opened and Ben bounded out to greet them.

'Hi there.' Dante lifted Ben high in the air and felt small arms wrap round his neck.

'You're back!'

Taylor crossed round the vehicle and watched as Ben swivelled in Dante's grasp to reach out and plant a kiss on her cheek.

'I missed you.' He scrambled down and caught hold of her hand. 'Did you have fun?'

'We had a nice time,' she assured solemnly. 'We visited the markets, and went out to dinner.'

They moved as a group indoors, where Graziella welcomed them with fond affection.

'Lena will bring tea out onto the terrace in half an hour. That will give you time to unpack.' She spared Taylor a warm smile. 'I've had Lena transfer your things to Dante's suite.'

'Thank you.'

'Can I come and help you unpack?' Ben asked a little wistfully, and Taylor gave his hand a reassuring squeeze.

'Of course.'

The suite Dante occupied was large, the bed king-size, with an adjoining *en suite*, double walk-in wardrobes, and visible through a wide aperture there was an informal room furnished with a comfortable sofa and chairs.

Dante followed soon after with their bags, and Ben perched on the side of the large bed.

Taylor was almost done when Ben announced in a sad little voice, 'I had a bad dream last night.' He was trying to play it down, but not quite succeeding, and she crossed to his side to sit beside him. 'I dreamed you didn't come back.'

Her heart turned over, and she gathered him close. 'It's OK,' she assured gently.

'Daddy and Mummy were going to come back, but they didn't,' he said in a quiet little voice.

'There was an accident, sweetheart.' She felt the tears welling in her eyes, and blinked rapidly to dispel them. 'A car accident, you know that.'

'Yes, but why? Daddy was a good driver. Just like Dante.'

Dante hunkered down to Ben's eye level. 'Will it help if I promise to be very careful?'

Ben looked incredibly solemn as he considered Dante's words. 'Some,' he admitted. 'I guess.' His shoulders moved as he took a deep breath. 'I cried, and Nonna came and got me. Nonna told me a story and I fell asleep.'

Taylor's heart felt as if it broke a little. 'Well,' she began quietly, 'tonight you get *two* stories.'

He brightened a bit. 'Can I pick them? One from you and one from Dante?'

'Sure can.' She lifted his hand to her lips, and smiled. 'How about you come see what we bought you?'

'A present? You brought me a present?'

Dante rose to his full height as she scooped Ben into her arms and moved to her bag.

'It's only small, but I think you'll like it.' She withdrew the box with its bright wrapping, and watched as he carefully undid it.

He was a lovely little boy, gentle in the ways that counted, and she felt so fiercely protective of him it almost brought her to tears.

The wrapping came off, he lifted the lid…and smiled. As she'd predicted he would when she purchased the small black porcelain kitten.

'It's just like Sooty. There's the same white splash on his nose.' He hugged her tight. 'Do you think he and Rosie will have missed me?'

'I'm sure they have.'

Graziella was about to serve tea when they joined her, and afterwards Dante excused himself to go check the vineyard and cellars.

It looked like being a bumper harvest, and there was a sense of pride in that it was his…a place where he aimed to spend more time as the years progressed. His private niche to escape the pressures of big business and discard some of his obligations.

He'd acquired a wife, and soon he'd be able to call Ben his adopted son. The next d'Alessandri generation was secure.

There was a need to be part of it…except he was due in Paris tomorrow; Wednesday they'd depart the vineyard for Graziella's apartment in Florence; Thursday he would take the early flight to Rome; Friday he'd need to wrap up business matters in the Florentine d'Alessandri office; a gala event in the city necessitated his presence Saturday evening; and Sunday he would return to Sydney with Taylor and Ben.

A full schedule, but a necessary one in order to keep his finger on the pulse of the d'Alessandri corporation.

It was evening when he returned indoors and went upstairs to shower and change for dinner. Taylor had chosen a stylish design in varying shades of pink, and he voiced his appreciation as he admired the way her fingers deftly fixed her hair.

For a moment he almost suggested she leave it loose, but then he wouldn't have the pleasure later of removing the pins and letting her hair cascade down onto her shoulders.

'Ben?'

She shot him a glance via mirrored reflection. 'With Graziella.'

He began undoing the buttons of his shirt, then pulled it free and shrugged it off.

She loved the shape of his back, the way it curved up to his shoulders, the strong musculature that seemed to flow fluidly with every move he made.

Olive skin, lightly tanned from his days in the sun, and the tapered waist.

She had an urge to close the distance between them, lean in close and curve her arms round his shoulders, then angle her mouth against his own.

Instead she returned her attention to her hair, and focused on applying lipgloss as he stripped and walked naked into the *en suite*.

Dinner was a relaxed meal, after which they saw Ben into bed, read the promised two stories, after which Dante indicated the need to spend time in his home office.

'That's OK,' she assured with a smile. 'I'll take my laptop down to the library.'

Why should this evening be any different from those preceding it?

Their marriage wasn't a love match, she reminded herself as she retrieved her laptop and made her way downstairs.

So…forget any fanciful feelings, and accept that life after marriage wouldn't be much different from how it had been *before*.

Except she now enjoyed the wonderful bonus of intimacy…with a man whose sexual skills proved delightful beyond belief!

Taylor worked until the letters on-screen began to blur, then she saved the file, closed down and quietly made her way upstairs, checked on Ben, then crossed to Dante's suite.

Empty, she perceived as she quickly dispensed with her clothes and slid into bed.

She fell asleep within minutes of her head touching the pillow, and she wasn't aware of the man who joined her some time later, or that she barely stirred when he gathered her close.

At some stage she became caught up in a series of dreams that merged and became one…sighing a little as light fingers brushed her thigh, slid over her hip and captured her breast.

'Nice,' she murmured…and almost purred with

pleasure as lips caressed the vulnerable hollow at the edge of her neck.

Fingers stroked the peak of one breast, arousing it to sensitive life, and she groaned a little as a hand trailed to her stomach, then moved lower to explore the incredibly sensitive labia...until she wanted to beg he ease the excruciating sensation arrowing there.

Then her body arched as he touched her clitoris, and she did cry out as he brought her close to orgasm.

The feeling was so intense, it brought her to wakefulness, and the dream became reality as Dante took possession of her mouth.

What followed became a feast of the senses, as he drove her high time and again, before joining her in a cataclysmic climax that left them both breathing deep and slick with sexual heat.

Together they lay there, easing down to a state of inertia.

Then Dante's watch beeped an alarm, and he moved from the bed, scooped her into his arms and strode into the *en suite*.

'What are you doing?'

'Having you share my shower, then I'll tuck you back into bed while I dress, have coffee, then drive in to the airport *en route* to Paris.'

'Paris?'

He opened the shower cubicle, turned the water dial, then stepped in and let her slide down onto her feet.

'Uh-huh. I'll be back tonight.'

Taylor reached for the soap and he took it from her, then began smoothing it over her body.

'What are your plans for the rest of the week?'

'Shower talk?'

'We've already done the sex thing.'

Dante lowered his head and kissed her...thoroughly.

'So we have.'

'Yes, well...it was nice,' she managed with circumspection, and heard his soft laughter.

'Rinse off, and go.' Dark eyes gleamed with amusement. 'Or I'll be tempted to show you better than *nice*.'

'You have a flight to catch,' she reminded.

'There's always tonight.'

She escaped, dried off, then she pulled on

underwear, jeans, added a top, then brushed out her hair and smoothed its length into a pony-tail.

He emerged as she moved towards the door. 'It's barely six.'

'So I'll go make coffee.'

'And kiss me goodbye?'

She pretended to consider it. 'Maybe.'

Dante the vintner was replaced by Dante the so-phisticated, tough businessman in an expertly tailored three-piece business suit, crisp linen shirt and silk tie. A briefcase and laptop rested on the table, and he took his coffee hot, black and strong.

It was he who laid his mouth on her own in a brief, hard kiss, then he collected both briefcase and laptop, shot her a dark, gleaming look, and left.

Taylor heard the four-wheel-drive start, followed by the muted hum of the engine, and she cleared their cups, then returned to their suite to sit cross-legged on the bed as she booted up her laptop.

Following breakfast she spent the day with Ben, then began packing ready to return to Florence the next morning.

Dante rang late afternoon to say he'd be

delayed and would arrive late, and on the pretext of a headache Taylor excused herself soon after settling Ben to bed.

She was unaware what time Dante returned, and when she woke next morning the bedcovers were tossed on his side of the bed, his pillow askew and the bed empty.

Graziella's apartment in Florence seemed constrained after the villa's spaciousness, and there was no room for Ben to play, which meant a more concentrated effort to entertain and keep him occupied.

Dante's presence seemed fleeting, for he spent nearly all of his waking hours tending to business, and on the few evenings he made it back to Graziella's apartment for dinner he retreated soon afterwards to put in long hours on his laptop.

If he was home in time he settled Ben into bed with a story, and Taylor used the evening hours to work, choosing to sit cross-legged in bed as she keyed the pages.

Twice he reached for her in the early dawn hours, after which they shared a shower, shared coffee, then he left for the city office.

Saturday proved to be just another day, although he gave Graziella his word he'd return in time to attend the evening's charity event.

Taylor was in the guest suite putting the finishing touches to her make-up when she heard Graziella offer several firm words and Dante's response.

Then he entered the suite, discarded his clothes in record time, showered, shaved and dressed in evening clothes, added a black bow-tie and pocketed his wallet, the embossed invitation, then he crossed to her side and took possession of her mouth.

'And that was because?'

'Just...because.' He touched a finger to her slightly swollen lower lip.

The inner-city hotel venue hosted a large number of guests mingling in the expansive marble-tiled foyer adjoining the ballroom.

A prestigious fund-raising event to aid children with disabilities, Dante relayed, and one to which the d'Alessandri corporation gave support.

Black tie among the men appeared *de rigueur*,

and the women wore designer gowns and sufficient jewellery to warrant tight security.

Taylor stood at Dante's side as she observed the guests. Much could be gained by idly noting stance, facial expression and mannerisms, she mused. It was an instinctive pastime of any artist engaged in creativity, the conscious and unconscious study of people, places, enhancing a developed sense of mood, ambience...the ability to stretch the imagination and take it to another level.

Voices, some muted, others bright, even extrovert, rose above the background music, and Taylor was fascinated by the tone and cadence of another language...one, if they were to spend any time in Italy, she and Ben would need to become conversant with.

Dante's recent marriage resulted in a series of congratulations by several guests, and Taylor smiled, inclined her head and intoned *grazie* at regular intervals.

Beautiful women, exquisitely gowned and groomed to perfection, whose greetings were a little too blatant...or was that just her fertile imagination?

Whatever, it gave her pause to wonder just how many associations Dante had enjoyed, and with whom.

'You seem to have a legion of female friends,' she managed quietly as a gorgeous— *gorgeous* was the only word—young woman moved away after offering him an overly enthusiastic greeting.

His dark eyes seared hers, and his mouth curved a little in silent amusement. 'It bothers you?'

She offered him a bright smile. 'Why should it?'

At that moment the ballroom doors opened and the guests were encouraged to show their tickets prior to being directed to their reserved tables.

Dante curved an arm along the back of her waist as guests converged, and there was little she could do to still the slow-curling sensation settling low in her stomach.

He generated a devastating sensuality beneath the sophisticated façade…a dramatic elemental quality that hinted of the primitive, as well as the passion.

A man who could drive a woman wild…and did, with superb finesse.

As CEO of the d'Alessandri corporation, Dante had earned the respect of many, and the woman he'd chosen to marry garnered speculative interest.

Media coverage ensured the populace in general were aware of Leon's tragic death, his orphaned son. It wasn't difficult to conclude Dante's recent step into matrimony very neatly took care of a few legal loose ends.

So why attempt to pretend the liaison was based on affection?

For Taylor it was more, so much more than she cared to analyse, and she was all too aware of the danger in mistaking affection for love. For to lose her heart to Dante would amount to emotional suicide.

'Caro!'

If it were possible for a feminine voice to *purr* and project provocative eroticism in the sound, then the woman achieved it…in spades.

Taylor was blatantly ignored as a female vision of perfection wrapped her arms around Dante's neck and kissed him…thoroughly.

There was a slight distinction in that he didn't

appear to participate and, to give him credit, he quickly released himself from her grasp.

Taylor had little knowledge of the woman's petulant response in French, but, accompanied by a moue, it was easy to do the maths.

'English, Simone,' Dante rebuked as he drew Taylor forward. 'Allow me to introduce my wife, Taylor.'

Beautiful, exquisitely showcased dark eyes glittered as Simone attempted to recover her poise…and her manners.

'*Wife, caro*?' The smile was a mere facsimile. 'I spend a month in Provence, and in that time you *marry*?' She spared Taylor a sweeping inter-rogative appraisal, and arched a perfectly shaped eyebrow. 'Really. How—' she pretended to search for the appropriate word 'extraordinary. Especially when Taylor did not number among your—' there was a delicate pause 'known— *acquaintances*, shall we say?'

'I have many friends, some of whom are women,' Dante drawled with silky smoothness, appearing not a bit disturbed.

'Some more special than others, *n'est-ce pas*?'

He merely offered a lazy smile. 'If you'll excuse us?'

'That was interesting,' Taylor commented as he led her in the direction of their allotted table. 'Not, of course,' she assured with deliberate guile, 'that I'd think of questioning your—er—active past.'

His husky laugh sent the blood fizzing through her veins, and she looked at him in silent askance as he lifted her hand to his lips.

Their table held prominent position, their fellow seated guests charming, with one vacant chair remaining.

The overhead lights dimmed a little in sequence as spotlights illuminated the podium, and Taylor focused on the charity chairperson as she addressed the guests.

Interpretation was guesswork, at best, although Dante relayed the gist of the speech when it concluded.

It was then Taylor noticed the empty chair had become occupied by Simone.

Dante's new wife and a former lover seated at the same table had to be someone's idea of a joke…or deliberate, to provide titillating speculation?

Taylor told herself she didn't care, as she indulged in polite conversation with deliberate ease, enormously relieved their table guests understood English.

Throughout the evening it became increasingly difficult to pretend she didn't notice Simone's clever flirting. It wasn't so much what Simone said, but the seductive tinge in her voice, the way her lips curved in silent invitation, and the deliberate slide of her tongue over her lower lip.

There was little doubt in Taylor's mind that Dante and Simone shared an intimate history, but flaunting it was nothing less than calculated intent.

If Simone hoped to engender some form of reaction, then she was bound for disappointment.

Taylor engaged a fellow guest in animated conversation about the plight of various Australian wildlife, comparing it to wildlife on other continents, as she valiantly strove to ignore Simone's antics.

It was crazy to feel upset, and she silently chastised herself for even beginning to care. What had she expected...her marriage to Dante to become a love match?

Get real. She was a mother for Ben, a social hostess and convenient woman in Dante's bed. Anything more belonged in the realms of fantasy.

Did he even have a clue how Simone's behaviour was affecting her? Probably not.

At that moment Dante covered her hand as it rested on her thigh, linked her fingers between his own and smoothed a thumb over the throbbing pulse inside her wrist.

Taylor turned her head slowly towards him, the flecks in her eyes a vivid green as she sent him a sparkling smile.

Then she did the unforgivable. She parted her lips a little and traced their outline with the tip of her tongue, glimpsed the sudden gleam in his dark, almost black eyes, before she turned away to continue her conversation with the conservationist.

The moment was compounded as the evening drew to a close and the guests began to vacate the various tables, for it appeared Simone seemed intent on aiming the final dart when she moved close to Taylor.

'You are a lucky girl, Taylor. Dante gave me the best sex I ever had.'

Without blinking, Taylor let her features break into a dreamy secret smile as she met Simone's glittering gaze. 'He's fantastic, isn't he?'

Dante turned at that moment, and his eyes narrowed fractionally as he caught Simone's expression. 'Anyone who chooses to upset Taylor will have me to deal with.' His expression didn't change, although only a fool would discount his words. 'Do I make myself clear?'

To give Simone credit, she merely smiled and, reaching out, she placed a beautifully lacquered nail on his forearm.

'Perfectly.' She turned gracefully, then glanced over her shoulder as she moved away. '*Ciao*, darling.'

'One of your conquests?' Taylor said as they began weaving their way towards an exit.

'An exceedingly brief and meaningless one.'

'You're not required to give me an explanation.'

His eyes darkened as they seared her own. 'You have my fidelity.'

She swallowed the sudden lump that had risen in her throat, and his eyes flared at the movement.

'Without question,' he added quietly, and it was all she could do to incline her head in ac-knowledgement.

It was late when they entered Graziella's apart-ment, and Taylor slipped off her stilettos as she moved quietly towards Ben's room, where she carefully pulled up the light blanket he'd kicked free, then, satisfied, she moved into the guest suite and began discarding her clothes.

Dante joined her as she pulled on her sleep top, and she uttered a startled gasp as he crossed to her side, caught the hemline in each hand and pulled it free.

His hands cupped her breasts, and they swelled in welcome, their peaks distending at his touch.

He leant forward and grazed his lips across her cheek, then sank to savour the sensitive pulse beneath her ear.

'What if I said I'm not in the mood?' Taylor said,

only to feel the breath hitch in her throat as he nipped her flesh, then soothed it with his tongue.

'You want me to prove otherwise?'

She contrived a negligent shrug, then gasped as he slid a hand between her thighs and sought the tender flesh there, to stroke and tease the acutely sensitised bud until she groaned for him to desist.

Fire, sweet and achingly hot, seared her flesh, and he closed his mouth over hers, smothering her faint cry as he sent her high, held her there, then sent her to another level where only his possession would ease the wondrous ache radiating through her body.

At this precise moment she didn't care, and she slid her hands inside his jacket and pushed it over his shoulders, then when it fell to the floor her fingers sought feverishly to deal with his shirt buttons, pulling the fine cotton free of his trousers before releasing his belt, the zip fastening of his trousers.

He took a moment to step out from them, then he placed a hand either side of her hips and lifted her high before positioning her to accept him.

Dear heaven. The faint sigh lay trapped in her

throat as she clutched hold of his shoulders and held on, exalting in the pressure of his thick shaft filling her and moving deeper with each pulsing thrust.

She moved with him, unaware he'd edged towards the bed, until he lowered her onto the mattress and followed her down.

There was only him, with her, as together they climbed the heights, held each other there, then fell in a glorious free-fall that left them breathing hard and slick with sensual heat.

For a while they simply lay there, bodies entwined in the tender aftermath as fingers drifted lightly over curves and hard planes; where lips soothed with such gentleness she almost wanted to weep.

Then Dante reached for the bedcovers and curved her close in against him.

His breath teased tendrils of hair at her temple, and she simply closed her eyes as the steady, rhythmic beat of his heart lulled her into a dreamless sleep…from which she woke to daylight and the tantalising aroma of freshly brewed coffee.

A shower, followed by a late breakfast and the need to pack.

Saying goodbye to Graziella was more difficult than Taylor imagined, and it was Dante who gave his assurance they'd return soon, Ben who manfully attempted not to cry as the taxi arrived to transport them to the airport.

CHAPTER TWELVE

THERE was something magical about flying into Sydney over the harbour with its many coves and inlets, the majestic span of the bridge and the famed opera house.

Home.

Taylor felt the pull of familiarity as she idly watched a tugboat lead an ocean liner towards its berth, and there was a ferry beginning its city crossing from suburban Manly.

Smaller craft lay fastened to moorings in coves dotted along the northern foreshore.

Blue skies with the merest drift of cloud, and the sun lent a sparkle to the harbour waters.

The Gulfstream jet veered over land, cruising at a low altitude as it drew close to the airport. Soon they'd land, disembark, clear Customs and

Claude would be waiting to drive them to Dante's mansion overlooking Watson's Bay.

'Do you think Rosie will remember me?' Ben asked as Claude eased the Mercedes out from the air terminal.

'Probably,' Taylor allowed with a degree of caution. A month's absence equated to a long time for a young puppy.

It didn't take many minutes before Rosie licked his hand and danced barking at Ben's feet, and Ben beamed as Rosie proceeded to shadow Ben wherever he went for the rest of the day.

Within a matter of days life had settled once again into a regular routine.

Dante left early each morning for the city office and returned most evenings in time for dinner, with the occasional phone call citing a delay and not to wait up.

Ben returned to kindergarten three times a week, and Taylor sought seclusion in her allotted home office…and wrote.

On the two week days Ben was home, they spent time together at a park, attended his swimming lessons and Taylor supervised his practice swimming in the pool. Occasionally they visited a museum, watched a suitable DVD or took in a movie.

Dante joined them at weekends, and two weeks stretched into three…carefree days enhanced by Ben's ability to adapt to his life-changes.

The nights were something else. Sharing intimacy with Dante became an increasingly riveting experience…tactile, unrestrained, primal in the need to sate a hunger so intense it was almost frightening.

Mostly she managed to rationalise it was simply very good sex…and tamped down the longing for it to be more.

Love equated to wishing for the moon, stars and the entire universe.

Except…surely a man couldn't make love the way Dante did, and it not mean anything? Or was she merely a fool, too swayed by her emotional reaction to think straight?

Probably the latter, Taylor determined as she dropped Ben at kindergarten and drove down to Double Bay to meet Sheyna for coffee.

It was a lovely day, sufficiently cool to warrant

dress jeans, T-shirt, jacket and knee-length leather boots. However, the sun shone, and there was even a brisk breeze blowing in from the sea.

Finding a parking space wasn't difficult at this relatively early hour, and Taylor activated the locking mechanism on her car, then slipped the keys into her bag as she entered the coffee house.

It was easy to see the tall brunette rise to her feet as Taylor drew close to the table Sheyna occupied.

'Hey!' They shared an enthusiastic hug, then Taylor was moved to arm's length. 'Looking good, girl.' Dark eyes gleamed with wicked humour. 'Getting good sex becomes you.'

'And you know this…because?'

Sheyna rolled her eyes. 'Your husband has the look of a man who *knows* how to please a woman.'

Taylor lifted her hands, palms facing her friend. 'We're not going there.'

'Spoilsport.' Sheyna gave a philosophical smile. 'Shall we order?

'Now, tell me about Italy,' Sheyna begged as soon as they were seated. 'I bet it was fab.'

Taylor relayed much of the splendour of Florence, and her friend offered an envious sigh.

'Tell me you shopped and brought back heaps.'

'A few clothes, some gifts.' She reached into her bag and placed a slim wrapped box on the table. 'For you.'

'Really? You shouldn't have.'

'Open it.'

Sheyna took her time untying the ribbon and separating the sticky tape before removing the wrapping paper.

'Ohmigod!' The exclamation emerged as an almost reverent whisper. 'It's gorgeous. Perfect.' She slid the beautiful bracelet over her wrist and admired the delicate markings. 'Thank you.' She rose to her feet and placed an exuberant kiss to Taylor's cheek. 'You're an angel.' She settled back into her seat and leant forward, eyes intent. 'Now, how are *you*?'

One of the benefits of long friendship obviated the need for prevarication. 'OK. Ben is adjusting well. I'm getting there with the current book.'

Sheyna's smile was gentle. 'That's fine, Taylor, but I want to know about *you*. *OK* doesn't really cover it.'

'I miss Casey,' Taylor said quietly. 'So much.

I instinctively reach for my mobile to text her, only to realise she's no longer here.' She swallowed the lump that rose in her throat. 'A few days ago I found myself taking the route leading to the street where Casey, Leon and Ben lived, and I had to pull over and take a deep breath.' And still the flow of tears.

'Delayed reaction. Knowing you, you've been super-careful, pretending to be bright and cheerful for Ben's sake.'

'I guess.'

'Drink your coffee,' Sheyna bade. 'We're going shopping.'

'There's nothing—'

'You don't *have* to need anything.'

Taylor did her best to look vexed. 'You're impossible.'

Sheyna's mouth formed an impish smile. 'That's why I'm your friend, darling.' The smiled widened as she spread her hands. 'And where better to shop than *here*?'

Where boutiques sold only designer labels, and the vendeuse resembled a model out of *Vogue* fashion magazine.

She thought of her shopping excursion in Florence with Graziella in tow, the countless emblazoned designer bags they took back to the apartment...not to mention the diamond-encrusted wedding band that must have cost Dante a small fortune.

'I'll look, you shop.'

'Your husband heads a multi-billion corporation, and you're thinking *budget*?'

'A larger closet if I add any more clothes to it,' Taylor corrected, and caught her friend's indefatigable grin.

'Lingerie. A woman can never have too much.'

It was fun, Taylor decided on reflection, and good to relax and laugh a little. On impulse they indulged in a leisurely lunch, during which Taylor posed, 'You need to give me an update on Rafe.'

There was a telling silence. 'Sheyna?'

'He wants to marry me.'

'And you've said?'

Sheyna waited a beat, then a winsome smile curved her mouth. 'Yes, damn the man.'

Taylor returned the smile, then she broke into

subdued laughter as she rose to her feet and gave Sheyna an affectionate hug. 'I'm so happy for you.'

'There's more. My mother wants the works...me in a white dress, veil, a dozen bridesmaids, several hundred guests. You, my friend, will be there as matron of honour. I'll need someone sane to help me through this,' Sheyna finished with a shake of her head.

'Done,' Taylor said with delight. 'When?'

'Next year. Mother needs to *plan*!' She executed an effective eye-roll. 'I think we should elope. No fuss, *just do it.*'

'You're the only child,' she reminded gently. 'Your mother would never forgive you.'

Sheyna withdrew a cheque and placed it on the table. 'Five hundred dollars...you just need to fill in the name of the charity.'

Taylor picked it up and tore it in two. 'All bets are off. Just—be happy.'

They finished their coffee, then parted with the promise to meet again soon.

Ben ran to meet her when she collected him from kindergarten and he grinned with delight at the prospect of riding his bike at the park.

'Did Claude *really* put my bike in the boot?'

He climbed into his booster seat and she fastened the safety harness. 'Would I disappoint you?'

'You're the best.'

Taylor kissed the tip of his nose. '*Grazie.*'

They shared a fun few hours as Ben showed his prowess on the bike, the swings, the jungle gym, and to top off the afternoon she stopped off for ice cream on the way home.

Her mobile rang as they reached the car and she checked caller ID, saw it was Dante and picked up.

'Hi.'

'I'll be caught up with a few business associates, and late.'

'So don't wait for dinner,' she added. 'No problem.'

'Say goodnight to Ben for me.'

'OK.'

'*Ciao, cara.*'

It was almost eight when Ben settled to sleep, and Taylor took coffee into her home office, opened the laptop and worked on the current scene. This story was developing well, but, with the trip to Florence and everything that had entailed, progress was slow. For days Taylor had danced around the need to research certain police procedure, but any time soon she'd need to set up an interview with a professional and take notes. Writing suspense fiction required authenticity, and fudging it wasn't an option.

Soon she became immersed in the characters, heightening the tension, foreshadowing the event which would provide the hair-raising climax. Building on it, producing the words to portray the emotion, the fear, meant total immersion in the story, and she lost track of time, pausing only to read through her notes and check her facts.

She checked her watch, saw the time and began wondering how late was *late*. How many restaurants and bars remained open after midnight? And were there only business associates...or did they have feminine company?

Oh, for heaven's sake...stop it! You're overtired and verging toward overwrought. So go take a hot shower.

Except she felt the need to expend some

energy, and without further thought she took the stairs and crossed to the indoor pool. The door was locked, but she knew the combination, and minutes later she switched on the underground pool lighting, stripped down to bra and briefs, then dived in from the deep end.

The water was smooth and cool…too cool at first, although after stroking two laps the water temperature no longer seemed to matter.

Seven more laps, and she paused and reached for the pool's tiled lip with one hand and smoothed the excess water from her hair with the other.

It was then she saw Dante seated on one of the padded loungers. He'd discarded his jacket, his tie, and opened the top buttons of his shirt, released his cuff-links and rolled back the sleeves to mid-forearm.

'What are you doing here?'

He stood and slid hands into his trouser pockets. 'I could ask you the same question.'

'I felt like a swim.'

He watched as she smoothed a hand over her face. 'Are you coming out?'

'Not yet.'

Her eyes widened as he began unbuttoning his shirt, and she spluttered into startled speech when he reached for the belt on his trousers.

'What are you doing?'

Shoes, socks, trousers, then he removed his watch and moved towards her.

'Joining you.'

Seconds later he dived cleanly into the pool and swam underwater to surface beside her.

'You're crazy,' Taylor managed, then she gave a startled yelp as he captured her head and took possession of her mouth.

Possession was an apt description as he coaxed her response, then he plundered deep, hungry, compelling, almost branding her…then he eased back, gentling until his lips brushed her own.

'You chose the venue.' His voice emerged through a soft, musing smile, and she could only look at him through dazed eyes.

He angled her head, then touched his lips to each eyelid in turn. 'I can think of an infinitely more satisfying exercise.'

'It's late, and I'm tired.'

'In which case, it'll give me pleasure to do all the work.'

The next instant he moved easily from the pool, then reached down and pulled her up beside him. There was a shower stall with soap, shampoo and towels stored within easy reach, and he led her there, opened the water dial, stripped off his briefs, then reached for the clasp of her bra, freed it, and skimmed her bikini briefs free.

She wanted to protest when he took up the soap and began soothing it over her body, and she objected when he filched the bottle from its holder and massaged shampoo into her hair.

When he was done, he took a towel from her hands and wound it round her hair, then he used another to dry the moisture from her body.

'Your clothes,' Taylor reminded as they emerged from the shower stall, and she waited while he collected them.

'You sound like a wife.'

There was a teasing note in his voice, and she gave a light shrug. 'For better or worse, I seem to be yours.'

They ascended the stairs, and on entering the

master suite, he simply removed the towel from her body, discarded his own, then pulled back the bedcovers and drew her down onto the bed.

True to his word, he did all the work, savouring, teasing, tasting...until she clung to him, urging his possession.

It was violently sweet, sensual and tender... so much so, it was almost more than she could bear.

Sunday was allocated as a family day, and Ben chose Taronga Park Zoo for their excursion.

Spring was in evidence everywhere, Taylor noted as the Mercedes traversed suburbs beneath Dante's competent hands.

There were pink and white blossoms appearing on fruit trees, and gardens bore the emergence of colour beneath warm sunshine and almost clear blue sky.

A slight breeze teased green leaves on many tree branches, and tall city buildings directly across sparkling harbour waters provided a panoramic vista as the Mercedes slid into a parking bay.

'I love going to the zoo,' Ben enthused as he scrambled from his booster seat and jumped down onto the pavement.

'No running,' Taylor reminded, and he obediently took hold of her hand.

There was a muted beep as Dante electronically locked the car, and they walked together to the main entrance, paid and, once in the park itself, Dante swung Ben onto his shoulders.

'Wow, this is cool. I can see *everything*.'

They had dressed casually in jeans, topped with a shirt and jacket, with comfortable trainers on their feet. Layered, Taylor mused, to suit the season.

The zoo was well-populated, with groups wandering along the many paths as they paused to view the numerous exhibits. Tourists were digitally recording flora and fauna, the many Australian wildlife exhibits, with the red kangaroo, wombat and koala proving the most popular.

The Orang-utan Rainforest, the elephant enclosure, with the giraffes and zebras were right up there among Ben's favourite places to view.

By far the best, in his opinion, was the Free

Flight Bird Show in an amphitheatre overlooking the harbour.

Lunch was eaten alfresco, and they took the Sky Safari Cable Car.

Ben remained in his element as the day progressed, and Taylor took pleasure in his company.

Dante was something else. Tall, broad-shouldered, he bore the look of a high-powered tycoon in relaxation mode. For even attired in casual clothes, with shades and ball-cap he attracted interested glances.

She tried to pin it down, and couldn't come up with any one factor...more a combination of several. His fluidity of movement, stance, a deceptively calm persona that hid a steely ruthlessness with any adversary. Add sensuality and a compelling sense of passion...and the result was lethal.

Women looked...and wondered, while men conceded to varying degrees of admiration.

Taylor wore his ring, shared his bed, his home...and she knew that she also loved him deeply.

Attraction, recognition of something more,

sexual chemistry at its zenith…she'd fought them all, and lost. For Dante had made her *his* with seemingly little effort.

He cared…but *love*? The all-consuming, ever-after kind? Maybe that would come in time.

The afternoon was almost at a close, and there was a cool bite to the air…evidence winter wasn't quite done.

Taylor began turning away from the enclosure they were viewing and caught sight of a familiar male face…one she'd hoped never to see again, and she froze, hardly able to breathe.

Two years, yet his features were etched in her brain, for how could you ever forget the face of a man who'd launched such a vicious assault?

Even now, it crowded in on her, the sight, smell, and the fear.

Worse, that he recognised her too, and stood there, silently taunting her.

'Taylor?'

Dante's query barely registered, and he cupped a hand over her cheek as he subjected her to an intent gaze, noting her paled features, the stark expression in her eyes. 'What is it?'

She couldn't answer, for her voice seemed to be locked in her throat.

'You look as if you've seen a ghost.' He spared the area a searching look, and saw nothing to cause her reaction. Then his eyes narrowed, eliminating possibilities in rapid succession until there was only one.

'Is it him?' The question was softly voiced.

'Brown woollen jacket, navy blue beanie,' she managed in a stilted voice.

'Take Ben.'

Her eyes widened at the silky command, and she grasped Ben's hand, met the little boy's anxious expression, and sought to banish it.

'Shall we go take a quick look at the kangaroos?'

They hadn't long left the enclosure, and it was only a short distance away.

'Where's Dante gone?'

'He'll be back soon.'

It didn't seem long before Dante rejoined them, and there was little to determine from his expression. He placed a hand on Taylor's cheek before swinging Ben up onto his shoulders and leading them all back to the car.

Sunday evenings involved a dinner treat, given it was Anna's day off, and they stopped off at Double Bay, chose a child-friendly café and ordered a meal.

It was only later, when Ben was tucked into bed and asleep, that Taylor sought to query the outcome.

'You caught up with him?' There was no need to establish *who*, and it came as no surprise as Dante linked her hand in his as they descended the stairs.

Dante's expression didn't change, but his eyes assumed a quality she fervently prayed would never be aimed at *her*. 'You must know that I did.' Quietly and very concisely he'd explained he'd have the police reactivate Taylor's case and ensure he was brought to justice, endorsing the threat with a digital image on camera display as identification.

Her heart kicked in to a faster beat as he drew her close and lightly brushed her lips.

'I take care of my own.'

Words that made her feel warm, protected, and she realised that she did feel safe. She had done for a long time now and she knew that it was down to Dante. She parted her lips and lightly caressed his tongue before stepping away from him.

'You have work,' she managed with an impish smile. 'And so do I.'

He stroked a light finger down the length of her nose. 'You'll keep.'

It was later…much later, when Dante entered her home office and regarded the slight droop of her shoulders as her fingers flew across the keys.

'Enough, Taylor. Save the work and close down.'

She glanced up from the screen. 'When I finish this paragraph.'

'Five minutes.'

She was done in four, and she entered their suite a few steps ahead of him, divesting her clothes in quick, economical movements, aware he mirrored her actions.

Taylor caught up her sleep top and had pulled it part-way over her head when warm hands covered hers and tugged the top free.

'What—?'

'You won't need it.'

He didn't offer another word as he placed a hand beneath her knees and carried her into the *en suite*…where, she saw at once, he'd filled the spa-bath and set the temperature to warm.

'Decadent.' Delicious, she added silently, and gasped a little as he stepped in with her in his arms, then sank down and pulled her to sit between his thighs.

Heaven, as the water started to pulse, and she sighed with pleasure as he began to massage her shoulders, easing out the kinks.

It was all too easy to simply close her eyes and let her mind drift.

Precisely his aim, as he sought to ensure she was sufficiently relaxed so she slept undisturbed, with no dark memories surfacing to tip her into a nightmare.

Hours before, it had taken all his control not to put a fist in her assailant's face. Icy rage, such as he'd never experienced before, consumed him, and he'd gained a small degree of satisfaction as his threat had hit home.

He possessed the most beautiful hands, Taylor mused as they soothed and caressed, and she let her head fall back as his lips sought the vulnerable pulse at the base of her throat.

Gentle fingers teased the peak of each breast, then slid low to seek the throbbing pleasure pulsing at the apex of her thighs.

He took his time, gently easing her high, holding her there as she arched against him, then he used his mouth in a flagrantly erotic kiss while he absorbed the cry as it rose in her throat.

Again the waves of sensation radiated through her body, and she twisted her head and nipped his shoulder with her teeth.

With a husky sound he lifted her to face him, watching her expression as he positioned her to accept him, glimpsed the way her eyes dilated, saw the moment she went blind as her orgasm consumed her, then he covered her mouth with his own, savouring her pleasure and taking his own.

Afterwards he cut the pulsing jets, then lifted her onto the tiled floor, filched a towel and dried her, himself, then he took her to bed, curled her close, switched off the bedside lamp…and held her through what remained of the night.

CHAPTER THIRTEEN

WEDNESDAY morning Taylor unclipped the safety harness on Ben's booster seat and lifted him out from the car.

'We're doing finger-painting today.' Ben's smile stole into her heart and rested there. 'It's going to be fun.'

Together they crossed the parking area and entered the brightly decorated hall, greeted one of the teacher's assistants, then Taylor accompanied Ben to the cloakroom, watched as he hung his small backpack on his name-designated hook, then followed him to a group of children.

'Bye, sweetheart.' She sank down to his eye level and gave him an affectionate hug, felt the small arms wind round her neck and kissed his cheek. 'See you this afternoon. Have a great day.'

He offered a happy grin. 'You, too.'

Taylor waited the few brief minutes to ensure he was happily ensconced, then she acknowledged the teacher's assistant before crossing to her car.

Clouds were rapidly banking up across the skyline, and within minutes rain splattered the windscreen, then rapidly changed into a hefty downpour.

Great. Hopefully by the time she reached the inner city, the worst of the rain would have lessened.

It didn't, and the few free allocated parking bays adjacent the police station were already taken…which meant circling the block, then the next, before she slid the car into a vacant bay.

Fortunately she'd allowed ample time before her interview appointment, and an umbrella shielded her from the worst of the rain as she covered the distance.

Police stations were mostly functional, a little battle-scarred, and this particular one in a less salubrious inner-city suburb definitely showed signs of wear and tear.

If she'd wanted modern, she could have chosen a station elsewhere.

All it took was a quick glance to realise the reality matched her quest for atmosphere.

And then some…For the waiting area hosted a few men in various guises, one so heavily bearded and bearing tattoos on what appeared to be every visible area of skin. There were also four women, two of whom looked to be in their late teens, their attire garish, extreme, wearing heavy make-up and sporting bed-hair.

Grunge was the order of the day, with the odour of stale alcohol and cigarette smoke seeping through the inadequate veil of cleaners' antiseptic.

She'd deliberately dressed low-key in jeans, with a jacket worn over an open-necked blouse, and kept make-up to a bare minimum.

Taylor waited her turn, then stated her appointment time and with whom to the officer behind the counter. She saw there were no vacant chairs and so stood to one side to wait.

The shoulder-bag held a mini tape recorder, spiral notebook, pens, and a comprehensive list of questions…in duplicate…concisely written, so she could cram as much inside knowledge into the time allotted her.

All in the name of research.

Imagination was fine, internet research a credible tool, and film provided the visual. But nothing compensated for the opportunity to experience the reality.

Phones rang in the background, worn filing cabinets slid open and closed with increasing regularity with the constant ebb and flow of people signing in for whatever charged offence they'd committed.

A feminine voice raised in argument and peppered with explicit oaths rose above the cacophony of sound, together with that of an irate offender whose belligerence appeared to severely test the officer's patience.

Authenticity at its most vocal, Taylor mused as her writer's mind absorbed it all in detail.

Minutes later the outer door swung open and a lean, mean-looking male in his twenties shuffled towards the counter.

He wore shabby-chic low-waisted jeans, a leather jacket over a T-shirt, a kerchief knotted at the back of his head and trainers on his feet, though it wasn't so much the apparel but his burning, wide-eyed stare that lifted the hairs on the back of her neck.

It soon became apparent taking his turn held little appeal, something about which he became quite vocal, although he quietened at a harsh directive from the officer manning the counter.

Two detectives emerged from a locked door guarding the entrance to a warren of internal offices, and exited the waiting room.

Taylor idly skimmed the many posters and notices pinned to almost every wall surface…information; penalties; warnings; phone contact numbers for the mentally, physically and sexually abused women suffering domestic violence.

Realism, in stark detail.

The guy with the kerchief began tapping one trainer against the linoleum, unable to keep still…needing, presumably, a fix of choice.

What happened next became a blur…one second he was seated, then he was in front of her, hands roughly dragging her upright, and a knife-blade rested a fraction of an inch from her throat.

Dear God.

Everything stopped…or at least it seemed that

way, for Taylor was unaware of movement or sound.

'All of you—out. *Now.*' The command was issued in a guttural snarl, and the waiting area cleared within seconds.

Had the officer manning the desk pressed a hidden panic button? Was there even one? Who knew?

She had the presence of mind to remain still. So too did the officer, as he began the psych thing, attempting to talk her captor down.

Two uniformed men emerged through the locked door and made a controlled effort to persuade him to give them the knife and let her go...whereupon he began shouting, vowing to kill unless his demand for a certain officer's presence was met...*now.* When he was told the officer wasn't on duty, the blade stung her throat and she felt the warm trickle of blood.

'*Get him here*, or I'll cut her again.'

The officer motioned he'd make the call, and Taylor watched as he keyed in a series of digits.

Think calm, focus. The words seeped into her mind, sharpening it. Reality was a different ballgame from practised self-defence moves under supervision. Except knowledge gave her an edge...slight, but with the element of surprise, she just might be able to provide a diversion.

She was in a police station, for heaven's sake! There was no better place to have experienced help on hand.

'Press the loudspeaker function.' The command was terse, angry, demanding. 'I want to hear his voice.'

The ringing tone sounded loud, and she used her captor's momentary distraction to sink her teeth into his hand, connecting with the bony joint at the base of his thumb. Simultaneously she rammed an elbow into his ribs, then used his body's momentum to put him on the floor.

Everything happened fast as two officers converged, cuffed and marched the guy through a doorway *en route* to a holding cell, and a woman in uniform led her into an office and seated her.

'I'm fine,' Taylor assured with as much calm as she could muster, caught the woman's quick smile as she opened a cupboard and extracted a first-aid kit.

'I'll just clean you up a bit before your husband gets here.'

Dante? They'd called him? Why? 'It's only a small nick,' she protested.

It was then she saw the blood on her hands, her T-shirt…and realised there were more nicks than she'd first thought. In fact, the one on her hand resembled a slash where the knife had caught her.

On cue, it began to sting…and the breath hissed through her teeth as a swab of disinfectant hit.

A cup of tea followed, another officer took a statement and then Dante was there.

Tall, forbidding, indomitable…appearing icily calm as he crossed to hunker down in front of her.

One look at the darkness in his eyes caused her to swallow convulsively. 'They shouldn't have called you.'

He lifted a hand and trailed light fingers down her cheek. 'I disagree.'

'I hope you weren't in an important meeting.'

A finger gently pressed her lips. 'Nothing is more important to me than you.'

Her eyes widened. Well, then.

'You didn't think to fill me in on today's prospective appointment?' Dante queried with deceptive mildness.

'You probably would have raised an objection.'

'Indeed.' At the very least, suggested a police station in a safer area, and ensuring she was accompanied there. *Madre di Dio*.

'It was just some research and I had an interview,' she explained. 'It should have gone as planned.'

'Except it didn't. And you haven't answered the question.'

'Probably,' Taylor admitted slowly, then added, 'eventually.'

He rested his forehead against her own. 'It hasn't occurred to you that I've just spent the worst twenty-five minutes of my life?'

His mouth grazed hers with a gentleness that melted her bones, then he rose to his full height. 'Let's get you out of here.'

'But, my research. I have an interview.'

'No,' Dante refuted quietly, 'you don't. Not here, not now.'

'I'm fine, Dante.'

'You're visiting a doctor's surgery to have him

check those cuts and ensure you receive the appropriate booster shots. Then I'm taking you home.'

'I have my car—'

'Which Claude will collect later.' He turned towards the woman officer. 'You don't need my wife for anything else?'

Taylor registered the woman's slightly awed expression, and knew just how she felt.

'No. She's good to go.'

Dante offered a faint smile. 'Thank you.'

The Mercedes was out front in a no parking bay, sans any ticket. Who would dare, in the circumstances, Taylor perceived as he saw her seated, then crossed to slip behind the wheel.

'I really don't need to see a doctor.'

'It's a given.' He shifted transmission and eased the car onto the road. 'No argument.'

'Would it make any difference if I did?'

He shot her a burning glance. 'None whatsoever.'

So she suffered the doctor's thorough checkup, the change in dressings, the booster shots. Sutures were vetoed in favour of butterfly strips, and an hour later they reached home.

'I need to change.' Dried blood on a T-shirt

was not a good look, and there were splotches on her jeans. 'I can manage,' she assured as Dante ascended the stairs at her side.

'I'm sure you can.' His voice was even. 'But you won't.'

Taylor spared him a quick glance as they entered their suite, and she opened her mouth, only to close it again as she noted the dangerous bleakness in his eyes.

'The jacket first, hmm?' He carefully slid each arm free, then tossed it onto a nearby chair. The T-shirt came next, and was eased over her head with equal care. 'Sit down, and I'll remove your boots.' A minute later he undid the button at the waist of her jeans, slid the zip down and slipped them off.

Being attired in briefs and bra added to her air of vulnerability, and her eyes dilated as he shrugged out of his jacket, discarded his tie, then freed the top few buttons of his shirt.

'Aren't you going back to the office?'

'No.' He reached for her, drew her close, then lowered his mouth over hers.

'Dante—'

'Just—allow me this, hmm?'

He was gentle, so incredibly gentle it almost made her weep, and his hands slid over her slender form, shaping the soft curves, the hard planes…as if he needed the reassurance her only injuries were visible ones.

When he was done he tucked her head against his chest and held it there.

'What possessed you to take on a drugged-up miscreant on your own?'

A shudder shook his large body, and the breath stopped in her throat for a few long seconds as she absorbed his reaction.

Dante d'Alessandri…in shock? Because of *her*?

'He wasn't listening to the officer, and when two others attempted to get close, he went into a rage.'

'And this encouraged you to risk your life?'

Taylor shifted her head back to look at him. 'I didn't think so at the time.'

He shaped her head, tilting it. '*Cara.*' His eyes were dark, so dark they were almost black. '*Dio Santo*…what am I to do with you?'

'Next time—'

'There won't be a next time.' His voice was velvet-encased steel.

'I won't go alone,' she concluded, and glimpsed something in his expression she didn't even dare begin to believe as he traced the contours of her face, her lips with fingers that trembled a little.

If she did, he vowed silently, it would be over his dead body.

'Promise,' Taylor added, and saw him incline his head. 'And I'll be up-front and tell you where, when and why.'

'Wise.'

'I think I should put on some clothes.'

'Not quite yet.' His mouth touched hers, then sought the sensitive inner tissues, explored them, then he used his tongue to make love to her mouth with such eroticism she was in serious danger of melting into a puddle at his feet.

When at last he lifted his head, she could only look at him in a state of dazed confusion.

'The thought of losing you is more than I could bear,' Dante vowed softly.

Her mouth moved, but no words came out. Warmth coursed through her veins, flooding her body, and she was barely conscious of drawing breath.

'Each time we made love.' He paused as he took in the look of wonder encompassing her expressive features. *'Per meraviglia*...how could you not know?'

Still the words remained locked in her throat. 'I thought you were very good at sex,' she managed at last.

'Believe me...it was never just sex. I wanted *you*. Your heart and soul...all of you. Everything you are.'

She'd given it to him, generously, with a trusting heart...and imagined it meant little to him? *Santo cielo.*

'Taylor. *Inamorata.* I love you.' The words emerged as a selfless groan, and his eyes...

She thought she'd die from the way he looked at her. It was there...everything she'd ever imagined, hoped and prayed for.

Love. The enduring, everlasting kind. Naked and unmasked.

For her.

She swayed a little from the emotional impact, then gave a soundless gasp as he placed an arm beneath her knees and carried her to the bed, then joined her to regard her with concern.

'I'm fine,' she assured with a shaky smile. 'Just a little off balance from—' she faltered a little, then continued '—hearing what you said.'

'Words, *cara*?' he queried gently as he released the clip on her bra, then removed her briefs.

'Indulge me. I need to be here. Do this,' he vowed huskily. 'For both of us.'

With infinite care, he used his mouth to make love to her, caressing her lips, every inch of her face, the soft hollow at the base of her throat, each breast, their sensitive peaks, before tracing the scar at her ribs, her hip, then he trailed a path to her mouth and kissed her with such incredible gentleness her eyes shimmered with unshed tears.

He lifted his head, saw them and groaned, '*Cara*…don't.'

'You—undo me,' Taylor managed shakily. 'Always. Even before.'

Gentle fingers brushed her cheek, and his eyes darkened to the deepest chocolate and became liquid with emotion. 'Define *before*.'

'The first time I met you at Casey and Leon's

engagement party you made me wonder what it would be like to be made love to by a man such as you,' she admitted honestly. 'We lived continents apart, and I wasn't even on the same page as the women you dated.'

He captured her hand, lifted it to his lips, kissed each finger in turn…and watched the flecks in her eyes turn green.

'Then fate played a shocking hand.' It hurt to think of Casey and the tragic loss of two lives too young to leave this earth.

'Yet that same fate led us to *this*,' Dante reminded quietly. 'Love…and our future together.'

'With Ben.' All of a sudden her eyes widened. '*Ben*. He needs to be collected from kindergarten.' She started to rise, only to sink back as Dante rose from the bed.

'I'll go.' He lowered his head and kissed her. 'Tonight, *cara*, we pick it up from here.'

An hour later Taylor was seated in the informal lounge when Ben came bounding into the room with Dante merely a step behind him.

'Taylor! Are you OK?' He came to a stop at her side, his eyes large in his face as he saw the sterile strip taped to her throat, and another on her hand. 'Dante said you were hurt.'

She made light of it as she hugged him close, then she patted the arm of her chair. 'Tell me about your day. How did the finger-painting go? And where's yours? I want to pin it in my office so I can look at it when I work.'

It was enough to distract him, and afterwards they went down to the pool and she watched while Dante supervised Ben's swimming practice.

He was an incredible man. Powerful, passionate…and hers.

Soon she'd tell him how much she loved him, and she held the knowledge close as they sat through dinner.

'If you want to catch a few hours on the computer,' Taylor began as they quietly closed the door to Ben's suite after settling him to sleep. But Dante stilled the rest of her words by the simple expediency of placing a finger to her lips.

'We have something to finish, hmm?'

'We do?' It was fun to tease a little, secure in the knowledge that love bound them together…not convenience, or circumstance.

Love, the enduring kind.

He led her down the hall into their suite, closed the door, then drew her into his arms.

'Now, where were we?'

'Oh, I think here is just fine.' It felt so good to rest against him, to feel the beat of his heart, the potent warmth of his body, the touch of his lips as they brushed her temple...*knowing* how he felt about her added another dimension, one she'd do everything in her power to retain close to her heart.

'Is it so difficult to say?'

Taylor lifted her head and met the gentle softness apparent in his dark eyes, the wealth of love...just for her. 'No. I've searched for the right words, but none of them seem adequate.' She edged the tip of her tongue over her lower lip in an involuntary action. 'I love you,' she managed simply. 'The heart and soul of you. You're my life. Everything,' she added. 'All of it.'

'*Grazie.*' It slipped from his lips with heartfelt gratitude, and she smiled.

'*Prego.*' The simple acknowledgement resulted in an appreciative, musing gleam as he grazed his lips across her forehead, then trailed down to the edge of her mouth.

'*Per sempre,*' Dante vowed fervently. 'Forever, by the grace of God.'

Taylor melted into a thousand pieces, adoring him with all her heart. 'I think,' she said shakily as she framed his face and drew his mouth down to hers, 'we're about done with words.'

His soft laughter curled round her heartstrings and tugged. 'You think?'

Her mouth met his with a hunger that obliterated every last vestige of doubt.

MILLS & BOON PUBLISH EIGHT LARGE PRINT TITLES A MONTH. THESE ARE THE EIGHT TITLES FOR AUGUST 2009.

CR

THE SPANISH BILLIONAIRE'S PREGNANT WIFE
Lynne Graham

THE ITALIAN'S RUTHLESS MARRIAGE COMMAND
Helen Bianchin

THE BRUNELLI BABY BARGAIN
Kim Lawrence

THE FRENCH TYCOON'S PREGNANT MISTRESS
Abby Green

DIAMOND IN THE ROUGH
Diana Palmer

SECRET BABY, SURPRISE PARENTS
Liz Fielding

THE REBEL KING
Melissa James

NINE-TO-FIVE BRIDE
Jennie Adams

MILLS & BOON PUBLISH EIGHT LARGE PRINT TITLES A MONTH. THESE ARE THE EIGHT TITLES FOR SEPTEMBER 2009.

CR

THE SICILIAN BOSS'S MISTRESS
Penny Jordan

PREGNANT WITH THE BILLIONAIRE'S BABY
Carole Mortimer

THE VENADICCI MARRIAGE VENGEANCE
Melanie Milburne

THE RUTHLESS BILLIONAIRE'S VIRGIN
Susan Stephens

ITALIAN TYCOON, SECRET SON
Lucy Gordon

ADOPTED: FAMILY IN A MILLION
Barbara McMahon

THE BILLIONAIRE'S BABY
Nicola Marsh

BLIND-DATE BABY
Fiona Harper

MILLS & BOON